BROOKLYN

LEARNING TO WALK

BROOKLYN
LEARNING TO WALK

**THE COMPLETELY UNAUTHORISED FURTHER MEMOIRS
OF EVERYONE'S FAVOURITE TODDLER**

P.J. Smith

JOHN BLAKE

Published by John Blake Publishing Ltd,
3 Bramber Court, 2 Bramber Road,
London W14 9PB, England

First published in paperback 2002

ISBN 1 904034 40 3

British Library Cataloguing-in-Publication Data:

A catalogue record for this book is
available from the British Library.

Design by Envy

Printed in Great Britain by
Bookmarque.

1 3 5 7 9 10 8 6 4 2

Papers used by John Blake Publishing Limited are natural,
recyclable products made from wood grown in
sustainable forests. The manufacturing processes conform
to the environmental regulations of the country of origin.

THE
STORY
SO
FAR...

Once upon a time in Celebrityland there lived a boy named David and a girl called Victoria.

They were born of humble stock but they were fair of face and the gods smiled upon them and invested them with Secret Powers.

And lo! David grew strong and handsome, and he was possessed of a magic left foot which smite the ball mightily and bent it like a banana in the game of soccer, which was a pastime invented by the rulers of the land to amuse the peasantry. And the masses were fair amazed by his wizardry and rose up with one voice and shouted: 'Go on, my son.'

Victoria grew up not quite so handsome, but she was fashionably thin of frame and she joined a troupe of travelling minstrels called the Spice Girls and led them in casting a spell over the land with the mystical chant: 'I'll tell you what I want, what I really, really want.'

And it came to pass that David and Victoria fell in love, and they were married and became known as Posh and Becks The Golden Couple, and they amassed riches beyond the dreams of *Hello!* magazine and lived in the many-roomed Beckingham Palace in the heart of Celebrityland, amid slow rolling hills and fast rolling chauffeur driven limos.

They begat them a son, Brooklyn, a prince among babies who was destined to wield the sword of celebrity and become The Most Famous Toddler in Britain. And Brooklyn took up crayon and parchment and began a daily diary of their fairy story lives so that future generations could share the wonder of it all.

JULY
2001

Sunday July 1st

Ah, this is more like it! We've finally moved into Beckingham Palace – a mansion more suitable for a Superstar like myself, amid luxurious surroundings totally befitting The Most Famous Toddler in Britain.

This place is huge – three-and-a-half million smackeroonees-worth of prime Hertfordshire real estate. The driveway is so long that Little Chef want to build a restaurant on it, in case visitors get hungry between the main gates and the front door.

The corridors stretch too far for little legs like mine so I've been getting around on my *Teletubbies* tricycle with the training wheels. It's like being an explorer, finding something new every day. So far the bathroom count is up to four, and I suspect there may be a couple more somewhere in the hinterland. In one of the bathrooms Mum has built a kind of shrine to some woman called Audrey Hepburn, with a giant picture of her on one wall. It's a neat idea and I am currently seeking space to erect a similar shrine to Bob The Builder. Yesterday I got lost in the West Wing and it took Mum two hours to find me. She's thinking of having me fitted with one of those ankle tags that criminals wear when they're out on parole, so she'll know where I am at all times. I don't know why she got so frantic. She could have just phoned me on my mobile.

Monday July 2nd

The house has even got a library and Dad has put both his books in there. When he's finished colouring them, he's going to get another one.

My room is very tastefully done, with a huge mural featuring Mum and Dad as Cinderella and Prince Charming (I notice that Mum's glass slipper carries the Gucci logo). It's also got a really cool ceiling studded with fibre-optic stars, which changes like the sky, thanks to state-of-the-art projectors. A little ostentatious, perhaps, but then it is surely only appropriate that a twinkling little Superstar such as myself should have his own personal galaxy.

As I lie on my *Bob The Builder* duvet, gazing up at my very own sky, I can't help thinking that The World of Brooklyn Beckham is not a bad place to be in.

Tuesday July 3rd

Wow, the grounds to this mansion are something else – big enough for Dad and me to have a great kick-about and, as the nearest fence is almost half a mile away, there is little risk of the ball going into next door's garden. Come to think of it, the lawn is about the same size as Old Trafford. Yesterday me and the garden gnomes beat Dad 14–7. Mind you, I must admit that we got three of our goals while Dad was taking his shoes and socks off so he could carry on counting once the score passed 10.

Wednesday July 4th

Mum and Dad's anniversary, but they couldn't think of anywhere to go, which is understandable. What with us being The New Royalty, it's becoming increasingly difficult to find somewhere sufficiently exotic to cater for the capricious whims of a family whose tastes have been tailored by fame and fortune. Especially Mum. There was a time when she might have been tempted by a trip to Bali. But these days, her idea of a romantic setting is anything with diamonds in it.

Thursday July 5th

Boxes, boxes, nothing but boxes. We haven't finished unpacking yet (I'm still desperately trying to find my Ralph Lauren tracksuit with the monogrammed initials – if I go jogging with Dad, I want to look the part).

Still, I've had some great fun rummaging through all the clothes and playing dressing-up games. Mind you, Mum didn't find it all that amusing. She really went into one when she found me prancing around in a satin thong, diamond earrings and a silk headscarf with my nails painted silver. 'Brooklyn!' she screeched, in her well-known impersonation of a demented barn owl. 'Take them off at once. What have I told you about playing with Daddy's things?'

Friday July 6th

Mum continues to be paranoid about publicity, even more so now that we have moved down south and are closer to The Vultures of Fleet Street. As Dad came in from his morning run today, Mum asked him if there were any Press photographers lurking about outside. When he said there weren't, Mum threw a right wobbly.

'Maybe they haven't got our new address,' she said. 'I'll get my agent to phone the *Sun*, so they can send a couple of their cameramen to lurk about in the bushes. It just don't feel right not having the paparazzi invading your privacy.'

Saturday July 7th

Oh dear, experience tells me that Mum's fretful behaviour and worry about becoming

The Forgotten Face of Showbiz can only mean one thing: she's got a new record coming out. Aaaargh! Pass the earplugs!

Sunday July 8th

To the Prince Edward theatre with Mum and Dad to see the ABBA musical, which features strange, long-haired Swedish people in flared trousers. The audience went wild when they saw me, even though we crept in after the show had started so as to avoid such inevitable adulation. Anyway, they were all shouting and cheering and I think Mum and Dad, who were standing behind me in the royal box, felt quite left out. But they brightened up when the cast, who must have realised we were in the audience, finished the show with the Beckhams' national anthem and Mum hummed it all the way home in the limo: *Money, Money, Money ...*

Monday July 9th

One might think that the leafy hedgerows of Hertfordshire would help provide some sanctuary from the menace of The Big Bad Evil Ginger One, whose sinister shadow haunts every waking hour of Mum's existence. This was, after all, one of the main reasons for moving here, in the hope that her ensnaring tentacles could be kept at bay by the M25. But no. The insidious onset of the Ginger One seeps through the sunlit panes of our tasteful mock Tudor double-glazing in the form of a newspaper article that says the insufferable Spice Monster is planning a new career in films.

'Why not?' sniffed Mum. 'If she grew two more legs she could get a part in a Western.'

Tuesday July 10th

Found Dad sitting at a table chewing on a crayon. He was struggling to fill in a form about the local council tax. One question was: 'Length of residence in Hertfordshire.'

Dad put down: '500 yards.'

Wednesday July 11th

Dad has finally shaved off that ridiculous Mohican haircut, which is a huge relief to us all. It was somewhat scary being kissed goodnight by a Geronimo lookalike and I had nightmares about being scalped as I slept. One night I dreamed I was on a wagon train and Dad was leading a bunch of marauding Indians who were attacking us. I woke up to find I'd formed the pillows into a circle.

My greatest fear was that he would impose a similar outrageous style on my good self. For a start, it would seriously unbalance any future game of Cowboys and Indians I wanted to play with visiting chums, condemning me forever to end up on the losing side, as I would inevitably always have to play the part of the noble savage.

Anyway, Dad's had his head shaved and temporarily gone back to your average football-hooligan look until he decides what style he'll go for next. An anxious nation holds its breath.

Thursday July 12th

We've also been busy furnishing the place, and we are definitely not talking IKEA here. It's *Antiques Roadshow* all the way, and a designer called Nigel, who walks with a cat-like tread and sports a nice line in frilly shirts, has been called in to give advice. The place is beginning to look like a cross between Portobello market and the Palace of Versailles. Dad keeps asking why we have to keep buying all this old stuff when we could well afford something brand new. Last week Mum and Dad went to Sotheby's and bought a Louis XIV bed but when it arrived it was too small. So Dad sent it back and asked for a Louis XV.

Friday July 13th

In the meantime, Mum and Dad have bought a waterbed. As if that in itself wasn't naff enough, they've filled it with Perrier. It is quite disturbing at times to realise just how gauche my parents have become. Mum went to the doctor's the other day to have a small mole removed from her hand and the doctor said: 'I'll give you a local anaesthetic.'

'No you won't,' said Dad. 'We've got plenty of money. Give her something imported.'

Saturday July 14th

It's amazing how the baby years fall away and give place to the kind of new-found maturity which I am currently enjoying. Now that I'm talking really well I keep thinking back to those difficult days when I just couldn't get through to Mum, and each new word I spoke was received like a precious jewel. Every morning when she was dressing me I would point to the clothes closet and gurgle the same thing and Mum's face would light up. 'That's right, Brooklyn,' she would trill. 'Ah, mummy! Now, Brooklyn, say it again. Ah, mummy.'

Only now does she realise that what I was actually saying was 'Armani'.

Sunday July 15th

I just don't think people realise how style conscious babies can be, particularly when you are a Superstar like me. The first person to bring out a line of designer label nappies is on the way to a fortune. I mean, Pampers is all right as a brand name but it smacks of mass production and is not exactly the logo of exclusivity.

The constant battle for a fashion icon such as myself is to persuade one's parents that the toddler years need not be restricted to those vulgar garments such as snap-on romper suits, which put convenience before elegance. Last week in a Bond Street shoe shop Mum tried to impose upon me a hideous item of footwear known as a sandal, which I gather is quite popular among less discerning infants. Had I not kicked the assistant and screamed the place down, I could well be buckling on those crepe-soled monstrosities at this very moment. As it is, my monogrammed Adidas trainers with my initials and the tasteful gold stripes remain firmly in place.

Monday July 16th

Panic in the kitchen tonight. There was soup running down the front of our state-of-the-art inbuilt stove and splattering all over the Venetian tiled floor. 'Oh David,' wailed Mum. 'I thought I told you to notice when the saucepan boiled over.'

'I did,' said Dad. 'It was exactly 6.30.'

Tuesday July 17th

This part of Hertfordshire where we've moved to is much posher than Cheshire. Our local takeaway is a Kentucky Fried Pheasant. And at Christmas, the Salvation Army come around making a collection for any family with less than two swimming pools.

It is the ideal location for Super Rich Superstars such as ourselves, although Dad can never entirely put his working-class roots behind him. Only last week Mum had to severely reprimand him when he was seen talking to the dustmen.

Wednesday July 18th

It's just Mum and me for the next few weeks. Dad's off to Malaysia on a pre-season tour with Manchester United. Mum told him to send us some postcards, so he's taken a packet of my crayons with him. We had a final game of footie in the grounds and Dad took the head off a Grecian statue with one of his free kicks. We hid the head behind a bush and he told me not to mention it to Mum, but as the statue was an old one that had no arms anyway she probably won't notice that one more bit's missing.

My only fear is that while Dad is away Mum will seize the opportunity for some serious training in her bid to win an Olympic gold for shopping. Her 10-yard dash from the taxi to the Prada boutique has already been clocked at less than 5 seconds.

Thursday July 19th

Dad was never very good at geography, so when old Frosty Fergie, the manager, said they were going to the Far East, my old man thought he meant Essex. Mum's not much better. The other night at dinner, one of the guests asked her what she thought about Red China. She said it was all right as long as it didn't clash with the tablecloth.

Friday July 20th

Dad has always found travel somewhat confusing. Like, we went abroad on holiday last year and when we got back, one of Dad's mates asked: 'Where did you go?'

'I dunno,' said Dad. 'Victoria bought the tickets.'

Saturday July 21st

Be still my beating heart! Mum has invited the fragrant Baby Spice round for lunch tomorrow. What with the move from Cheshire and everything, it's been weeks since I have gazed upon her fair countenance, or felt the whispering touch of her lips against my eager little face, as she lovingly removes the candlesticks from beneath my nose with a delicately held Kleenex. Oh Baby Spice, I count the hours ...

Sunday July 22nd

Love lies bleeding.

Baby Spice was friendly enough but decidedly cool. The ardour, the passion, the intensity of our relationship has inexplicably gone. No longer does she sweep me to her luscious bosom, enveloping me in exotic smells, courtesy of L'Oréal (because she's certainly worth it) and cooing intimate endearments that only those in love could understand. This time round it was a quick grab of my cheek (which actually hurt) and a perfunctory kiss on the forehead. She didn't even bring me that bright-yellow Tonka bulldozer with the little man in the hard hat sitting in the driving seat that she promised me. Can it be that our love has fallen victim to The Curse Of The Spice Girls, which has wrecked so many lives in its maelstrom of envy, bitchiness, betrayal and revenge?

Monday July 23rd

As if the early symptoms of a broken heart were not enough to contend with, there was even more dismaying news today. Mum is releasing a new record called 'Not Such an Innocent Girl' and she goes round the house burbling the mind-numbing lyrics which have all the musical appeal of a nail being scraped down a blackboard. Honestly, she couldn't carry a tune if it had handles.

Tuesday July 24th

She's still singing that damned song. If Dad comes on the phone from Asia tonight I'll ask if I can fly out and join him.

Wednesday July 25th

On the other hand, I might just nip down to the local police station and apply for asylum.

Thursday July 26th

Tears mist my eyes and the droplets fall on your pages, dear diary, smudging the crayon and shattering my dreams. Scary Spice came round with Phoenix Chi this afternoon and I learned the awful truth.

Phoenix Chi: *Yo, Brookie-babes. How they hanging?*

Brooklyn: *Awful. I just can't get over how frosty Baby Spice was when we last met.*

Phoenix Chi: *Lighten up, my man. I don't know what you see in that chick. After all, she's been round the block a few times.*

Brooklyn: *Meaning?*

Phoenix Chi: *Meaning, sweetface, men. M–E–N, Blokes, geezers, eye candy, hunks. That sister is a man-eater. I mean, look at the guys she's dated. First* *there was that Spice Girls manager, then Rio Ferdinand the footballer, and she's had this big thing with this Jade Jones, the musician guy, like, forever. Let her go, dude. She ain't worth it.*

Friday July 27th

I keep going over things in my mind. The kisses, the cuddles, the Dinkey toys. And all the time the fragrant Baby Spice was seeing another. Treachery, thy name is love.

Saturday July 28th

The football season hasn't even started yet and there is already speculation that Dad might quit Manchester and join an Italian club. That would suit me fine – plenty of sunshine, La Dolce Vita and some serious shopping in Armani-land. However, the language might pose a bit of a problem for Dad. He thinks 'innuendo' is an Italian suppository.

Sunday July 29th

Mum's got this new album coming out and she has dedicated two of the songs to Dad: 'I Owe You' and 'Unconditional Love'. She insisted on singing them down the phone to him when he called from Thailand tonight. Yuk! I heard her tell one of her friends later that it really turned him on. If you ask me, the only thing it was capable of turning was my stomach.

Now, don't get me wrong. I love my Mum dearly. But, in her own interests I think she should seriously consider a change in career. I mean, her songs are bad enough when she has sound engineers, dubbing mixers, back-up singers and a 50-piece orchestra to help her out. Hearing her on her own is like standing outside a slaughterhouse listening to the bleating of a condemned sheep.

Monday July 30th

The most terrifying phrase in the English language must surely be: 'Let's make Brooky-Wooky a clean ickle boy then.' This is followed by a full frontal assault with a barbaric instrument of torture called a flannel, which is used to tear off the front of your face and then made into a point to scrape out your ears in a torturous process which should surely be brought to the attention of the Court of Human Rights. Is this brutality really necessary? Couldn't Mum just dust me down once a week?

Tuesday July 31st

Baby Spice The Deceiver had the cheek to come by again and, boy, was I Mr. Iceman. I turned my head when she tried to kiss me, which meant I got bright pink lipstick all over my ear, but I think she got the message. Now hear this, Baby. You and me are history, finito, endsville. You don't toy with the emotions of The Most Famous Toddler in Britain and think you can just carry on as though nothing had happened.

AUGUST
2001

Wednesday August 1st

Dad's back from Asia, and me and Mum returned from a shopping trip to Baby Gap to find him standing in the kitchen completely naked. 'I've made a Weight Watcher's salad,' he announced proudly. 'The recipe says: "Serve without dressing".'

Still, I must say he brought us some nice prezzies back from the Far East. I got a xylophone made out of bamboo and a very realistic looking rubber snake, which frightened the life out of the cleaning lady when I stuffed it down the loo with its head resting on the toilet seat.

Thursday August 2nd

Dad may not be the brightest bulb in the box, but there's no denying that he is pulling down some serious wonga these days, what with all the millions he's earning from advertising and endorsements. Last month he wrote a cheque and it was returned from the bank marked: 'Insufficient funds. Not yours. Ours.'

Friday August 3rd

Still, you have to wonder how a bloke like Dad has made it so big, considering that his whole life revolves around soccer and he doesn't know too much about anything except how to kick a ball. He thinks 'gross violence' is 144 Leeds United fans.

Saturday August 4th

Saw a group called Atomic Kitten on TV, and, wow, these are three heavy-duty ladies. They sing a song called 'Eternal Flame', and – ooh, yes – they can light my fire any time they want. I'm only just beginning to realise how much I was missing by being faithful to Baby Spice The Deceiver. My whole world revolved around her, and the idea of me even glancing at another chick was about as unlikely as Dad winning Mastermind. Phoenix Chi was right. A stud like me should put himself about more.

Sunday August 5th

I'm trying to decide which of the three Atomic Kitten chicks I like before I make my move on them. The one called Natasha is really top totty and just the kind of girl I need to obliterate all memory of you-know-who The Deceiver.

Monday August 6th

These days Dad is in demand to advertise everything from Pepsi Cola to trainers, and I sometimes wonder where he finds the time to actually play football. This morning I went with him to film a TV commercial at a Cheshire golf club in which he had to kick a football and hit a flag on the green from 80 yards. After five hours and countless attempts he still hadn't found the target, and I suggested to the director that I should have a go, since I was equally famous and at home had recently curled a beauty that took out several panes of the gardener's glasshouse. He didn't go for it, but fortunately someone had the bright idea of rounding up a group of golfers to form a wall in front of the flag. Dad bent the ball round them and managed to hit it first time.

This sort of advertising work is all pretty tedious stuff, especially when you think that at the end of the day it probably doesn't pay more than a quarter of a mil, but I suppose it gives Dad something to do until the season starts again.

Tuesday August 7th

I must say life has got a lot easier since people realised I am skilled in the art of conversation and no longer give me the goo-goo ga-ga treatment. It's taken more than 2 years for people to understand what I'm saying, even though I'm saying the same things now as I did when I was 6 months old. Why the hell grown-ups couldn't talk to me properly then instead of doing all that itchy-kitchy-coo crap is beyond me. However, since Mum and I have been in regular communication I now find that my name has been extended. It used to be plain Brooklyn. Now it's 'Brooklyn-stop-that-immediately'.

Wednesday August 8th

Have decided that Natasha from Atomic Kitten is definitely my kind of babe. I'll write to her as soon as I can get some of those sparkly stick-on hearts to decorate my *Bob The Builder* notepaper. I'll probably enclose a picture of myself dressed in my Batman outfit, which is, although I say it myself, pretty damned impressive.

Thursday August 9th

On the other hand, I think I'll borrow some of Mum and Dad's heavyweight headed paper with the twin golden crowns tastefully embossed on the top and Beckingham Palace picked out in raised Olde English type. That should convince her that I'm a classy kind of guy.

Friday August 10th

Some measure of Dad's position as a fashion

icon can be gauged by the fact that the other morning he was leaning forward into the bathroom mirror, mistook his forehead for his chin and accidentally shaved off half an eyebrow. For someone less famous, this might have been perceived as the actions of a prat. However, in Dad's case it is seen as a fashion statement and now half the young men in Britain are walking around with this cock-eyed, half-plucked look. I often think that if someone were to smack out Dad's front teeth with a billiard cue, the youth of the land would be rushing to the nearest dentist to emulate the look.

Saturday August 11th

Cancel that letter to Natasha of Atomic Kitten. Destiny has turned my heart in a different direction. Observe me closely. Do my hands not tremble, do my eyes not harbour the look of love? Dear diary, my emotions are in turmoil and I can write no more.

Sunday August 12th

Love is lovelier the second time around. Yo, you can say that again. Fragrant? This girl flourishes like marijuana at the Glastonbury Festival. I speak, of course, of Britney Spears, who I have just seen for the first time on the box. Forget that what-was-her-name from Atomic Kitten. We are talking here about one hot, foxy, top-shelf lady. Oh Britney, baby, where have you been all my life (I know that for most of yours I wasn't even born but, hey, who's counting?).

Monday August 13th

Wheee, what a weekend! We were up at the penthouse in Cheshire and on Sunday Dad got the Ferrari out and drove Mum and me to this brilliant place called Blackpool. I ate a load of candyfloss and ice-cream and fish and chips and Blackpool rock, and then we went for a ride on this big dipper thing,

which is really scary. I was spectacularly sick –
real diced carrots stuff – but nobody around
us complained because they evidently felt
privileged to be in such close contact with a
genuine Superstar, however smelly.

Afterwards we strolled along the prom and
Dad went to a mind reader. She charged him
half price.

Tuesday August 14th

Baby Spice The Deceiver has a new record
out called 'Take My Breath Away'. It's
obviously aimed at me, but she needn't think
I'll come running back. Sure, Baby, I'll take
your breath away. Just let me get my hands
on your throat.

Wednesday August 15th

England 0 Holland 2

Only a friendly, I know, but Dad wasn't
very happy and rightly so. Should a proud
nation that built an Empire really surrender

so readily to a country whose only claims to fame are cheese and windmills?

Thursday August 16th

Everyone knows that my Dad is the best footballer in the world but some bloke called Sir Geoff Hurst has written in the paper that Dad is 'overrated as a player'. Huh. Well, I don't know who this Geoff Hurst geezer is, but it's obvious he doesn't know a thing about football. He should try playing for England himself some time before shooting his mouth off.

Friday August 17th

Well, the natives are certainly friendly here in Hertfordshire, even though we do our best to keep them at bay with barbed wire fences, searchlights and guard dogs. The local Sawbridgeworth youth football team wants to sign me and has even made a shirt with my name on it. Yeah, all right, I know it's a publicity gimmick and they are just trying to cash in on the Brooklyn name. But if they seriously are looking for a player, they could certainly do worse than my good self. Last week me and the garden gnomes thrashed Dad 23–11. Mind you, it was Dad's turn to be referee and he sent himself off for a nasty sliding tackle on Grumpy with just 5 minutes left to play.

Saturday August 18th

The more I see of this Britney Spears babe the more I am convinced that she's tailor-made for me. She's only 20, but already she's one of the best-known chicks on the planet and she earns even more moola than my old man. She's worth more than £100 million smackeroonees, lives in an out-of-this-world fantastic Hollywood mansion and can make a simple pair of ripped jeans look sexier than a Liz Hurley frock.

Sunday August 19th

Manchester United 3 Fulham 2

Dad scored with one of his famous free kicks and to celebrate he took us for a hamburger. Outside the restaurant there was a bloke with a placard which said: 'Free Big Mac.' Dad went over to him and asked: 'Why, what's he done?'

Monday August 20th

It meanders through my mind like a silken stream in a sunlit valley. It caresses my very soul, like the brush of a petal across my dreaming eyes. Ah, that Britney voice! Was there ever a sound so sweet? You speak and the angels sing. All together now: 'Baby, One More Time!' Oh yes, baby. Oh yes!

Tuesday August 21st

Every time she opens her perfect mouth, the unforgettable Britney sends a clarion call to the lost and the lovelorn. 'Oops, I Did It Again,' sings the superlative Miss Spears and my heart leaps in time to the music. I asked Mum about her last night, but she just sniffed and said: 'Yeah, I s'pose she's awright.'

Awright??? We are talking here of the most divine creature ever to walk God's earth and my own mother dismisses her as 'awright'. Mummy dearest, Britney is not just 'awright'. She is perfect, flawless, a vision whose mere presence amongst us enriches my every waking hour. And what a pair of boobees!

Wednesday August 22nd

Put a football in front of my Dad and he is genius personified. Set him the simplest of tasks in the everyday world and he is just hopeless. For instance, sending Dad shopping is like getting a one-legged man to climb Mount Everest. Mum asked him to get me a packet of M&M's and when he got back he said: 'Sorry, they didn't have M&M's so I had to bring these W&W's.'

Mum gave him one of her what-are-you-like looks and said: 'David, these are M and M's. You had the packet upside down.'

Thursday August 23rd

Mum keeps talking about sending me to some place called nursery school and after that she wants me to go to some other gaff where they teach you to read and write. 'Education is very important,' said Mum. 'After all, if we couldn't sign our names we'd have to pay cash.'

Friday August 24th

I suppose she's right, really. Learning lots of things is important, especially when it comes to things like tying up your own shoelaces or reading the logo on designer clothing. Dad didn't get much of an education because he went to this really rough school in Essex. And when I say rough, I really mean it. The kids in the debating team were all on steroids.

Saturday August 25th

Dad says that the real problem was that the teachers at his school didn't know much either. The English teacher would insist on spelling 'taters with a 'P'.

Sunday August 26th

Lots of screaming, sobbing and kicking the kitchen cupboards today. No, not me, Mum. Some lady has written a book about her in which it says Mum is 'an average-looking woman with an undistinguished voice'.

I was tempted to say 'What's wrong with that?' but I sensed that the mood was not conducive to such a response, so instead I went to my room and watched that *Armageddon* video for a bit of peace and quiet. Knowing Mum, she'll probably calm down in a week or two.

Monday August 27th

More cupboard kicking and mutterings of 'average-looking woman indeed. How dare that illiterate little bitch say such things?' In the manner of a windswept sailor riding out a particularly violent storm, I snuggled beneath my *Bob The Builder* duvet and pretended to be asleep for most of the day.

It's a good job the cameras weren't around to film Mum's moodiness. She's making a documentary called *Being Victoria Beckham* and a TV crew has been following her everywhere. So where were they when she was Being A Pain In The Backside?

Tuesday August 28th

Everyone is making a big fuss because Mum wore a ring in her lower lip at a pop concert in Birmingham. I hope it's not a fashion she'll expect me to adopt. For a start, I suspect its installation would involve pain, which is not my favourite sensation, as I discovered early on in life when Dad accidentally ejected me onto a gravel path while trying to do wheelies with my push chair. Plus, a ring in your gob wouldn't half get in the way when you're sucking an ice-lolly or demolishing a Kit Kat. And if Mum plans to kiss me goodnight with that thing in place she's got another think coming. It would feel like getting mouth-to-mouth resuscitation from a curtain rail.

Wednesday August 29th

Mum also got booed at the Birmingham gig when her head mike fell off and people realised that she had been miming her songs. They should think themselves lucky. Every day in our house I have to listen to her actually singing.

Thursday August 30th

Dad's away with the England team in Germany and there's a big kerfuffle because their hotel in Munich is right next to a noisy beer hall which will keep them awake all night. I don't think there's much to worry about. Come midnight you won't be able to hear the oompah bands for Dad's snoring.

Back home, the team who are making the TV documentary wanted some footage of me playing in the garden, but Mum put the block on it. She said she didn't want me exploited. Cobblers! The truth is, she was frightened I would steal the show, but I didn't throw a wobbly or anything because I feel that it is my duty to help her ailing career as much as I can.

Friday August 31st

It turns out that the lip ring that Mum wore in Birmingham was only a clip-on thing that she wore for a bit of a joke. But this revelation came too late to stop several thousand girls rushing out to get their own lips pierced, amid much tut-tutting from the medical profession about health risks etc. Mum should have known better. As a trendsetter myself, I am very aware of the influence I wield. After all, it can be no coincidence that thousands of two year olds all over the country have followed my lead and stopped wearing nappies.

I well remember the effect it had when I first wore my *Teletubbies* T-shirt on *GMTV*. Kiddies' clothing stores were under siege and had to hire extra staff to cope with the onslaught of several million Brooklyn wannabees. Now I have been asked by all the major clothing retailers to alert them in advance to what I will be wearing on my various public appearances so that they may have time to prepare for the ensuing rush.

SEPTEMBER
2001

Saturday September 1st

Germany 1 England 5 (World Cup qualifier)

Engerrland, Engerrland! Pardon my hooligan-style chants, but my Dad's team has just stuffed the Krauts in spectacular style, giving rise to the sort of victory celebrations not seen since VE Day. Mum and I watched it on TV, with the cross of St. George flying proudly from the battlements of Beckingham Palace. 'Ee, aye, adee-o, who won the war?' (Mum taught me that one.)

The celebrations went on far into the night and I should not be surprised if the Queen declares tomorrow a national holiday and issues a special commemorative stamp.

Sunday September 2nd

Talk about national heroes! My Dad is being hailed as Captain Fantastic and the rest of the England lads are also being praised to the skies. Dad came home and celebrated in his own inimitable style by scoffing a whole packet of Jammie Dodgers (he was glad to see the back of that foreign food which they insist on serving in Germany).

Oh, and he came back with a German joke.

Knock, knock!
Who's there?
Guess.
Guess who?
Gestapo!

(The joke is considerably improved if you

deliver this response while slapping the other person round the face.)

Monday September 3rd

No more Jammie Dodgers for a while. Dad's back in training for the next World Cup qualifying match against Albania on Wednesday. Of course, Dad had no idea where Albania was but Mum, who is very much up on show business matters, volunteered the information that Norman Wisdom is extremely popular there. Which was useful.

Tuesday September 4th

As you know, we Superstars live with the constant threat of kidnapping, assassination or physical attack. Why, I myself had to be rescued from a howling mob outside Baby Gap just last week when over enthusiastic admirers made a grab for my *Bob The Builder* baseball cap. Bodyguards wheeled me away in my bulletproof pushchair, but it was a scary moment. I mention this because Mum said in an interview that she thought she was being targeted by a marksman at the Brit Awards last year, when she noticed a thin red beam of light pointing at her chest. I wouldn't worry, Mum. It was probably just The Big Bad Evil Ginger One glaring at you from backstage.

Wednesday September 5th

England 2 Albania 0 (World Cup qualifier)

One more win like this and Dad and the England team could be on their way to the World Cup in Japan. Oh gawd, what a thought. If Dad can't cope with sausages and sauerkraut in Germany, how's he going to get on with raw fish and live sea slugs in Tokyo? Plus, they eat with those chopstick things. Considering that Dad has only just about mastered a knife and fork, and still prefers to eat his Sunday dinner with a spoon, this could pose another difficulty.

Thursday September 6th

We are only just emerging from the annual Silly Season, a period where The Vultures of Fleet Street find themselves with very little to write about and are desperate for material with which to fill their so-called newspapers. Being Superstars, we Beckhams are constantly targeted as material to sustain their diet of sensation and drivel. I am a big enough celebrity to ignore such tedious tittle-tattle, but Mum is much more sensitive and she got all upset today when one rag dragged up all that old stuff about whether or not she is anorexic once again.

'There's nothing to be ashamed of in being anorexic,' said Dad. 'Lots of people get their words mixed up. I do it myself.'

'That's dyslexic, David,' said Mum. 'Anyway,' she said, 'I come from a thin family. My Dad weighed less than 4 pounds when he was born.'

'Amazing,' said Dad. 'Did he survive?'

Friday September 7th

Things can only get better. It turns out the divine Britney is still a virgin (another of those topics on which Phoenix Chi is so knowledgeable). Save yourself for me, Britney babe. Yeah, I know, Superstars like ourselves are constantly surrounded by temptation. But I can wait if you can.

Saturday September 8th

Mum still hasn't quite recovered from doing a disastrous concert in Leicester where I think the audience must have thought she looked underfed, because when she was finished some of them threw onions and apples at the stage. I was with her and if it hadn't been for my bodyguard heroically hurling himself across me I could have taken a direct hit from a Cox's Orange Pippin. As it was, I received a glancing blow from a Granny Smith and was almost caught in the crossfire of several carelessly flung shallots. It is not easy being on the frontline of fame, but I guess this is the price one has to pay for living in the trenches of celebrity.

Sunday September 9th

Despite his often bizarre taste in clothes, the more outrageous regions of which I thankfully do not share, Dad had been named by fashion experts as one of the world's top ten trendsetters, ahead of designers like Ralph Lauren and Giorgio Armani. Strangely, there is no mention of my good self in these awards, which surely casts serious doubt on the capabilities and good taste of those who sit in judgement on such surveys. Consider the occasion when I was pictured sucking on a bottle at Old Trafford. The very next day thousands of bottles were flung from high chairs all over Britain in a mass protest because they were not the same shape as mine. Need I say more?

Monday September 10th

It is inevitable that Superstars such as ourselves will attract parasites who see our enormous wealth as a target for their get-rich-quick schemes and dodgy propositions. An insurance man came to the house tonight and he was telling Mum how important it was that even very rich people like us should provide for the future.

'For instance, Mrs. Beckham,' he said. 'If your husband dropped dead tomorrow, do you know what you'd get?'

'Oh, yes,' said Mum. 'A Labrador. They're such good company.'

Tuesday September 11th

People keep telling me that the divine Britney already has a boyfriend, called Justin Timberhead, or something like that. But I'm not too worried. Destiny has decreed that Britney is mine, and I doubt that the path of true love will be blocked by some bloke whose name sounds like a store that sells outdoor clothing and hiking boots.

Wednesday September 12th

Mum's autobiography is due out soon and the fact that the publishers have already lopped £4 off the cover price is being seen as a sign that they are apprehensive about sales of this literary masterpiece. This is nonsense, of course, as the reduction is nothing more than a benevolent ploy to ensure that even the poorest and most underprivileged will be allowed access to this autobiographical gem whose inspirational story will quite rightly place the name of Victoria Beckham alongside such national heroines as Florence Nightingale, Emmeline Pankhurst and Dame Vera Lynn. The book is called *Learning To Fly*. 'Learning To Sing' might have been more appropriate.

Thursday September 13th

Mum and Dad took me to this brilliant place on the river called Runnymede where a bloke told us all about some historic document called the Magna Charta.

'When was it signed?' asked someone in the crowd.

'1215', said the guide.

'Blast,' said Dad, looking at this watch. 'We missed it by 15 minutes.'

Friday September 14th

After Runnymede we went on to Windsor, but we could hardly hear what the guide was saying because of the noise from the aircraft heading for Heathrow. Dad was really annoyed and said: 'You'd think they'd know not to build a castle so close to an airport.'

Saturday September 15th

Phoenix Chi came round and I was surprised to see her wearing a full Manchester United kit, complete with shinpads. She's very much into this Women's Lib thing and has joined a ladies' soccer team. When I told her the tight shorts suited her because she has a great pair of legs she belted me over the head with a Tonka truck and told me not to be such a male chauvinist pig.

I doubt if you'll ever find Mum joining a football team, though. She'd be horrified to think of appearing in public with ten other women all wearing the same outfit.

Sunday September 16th

I hid in the Wendy house all morning while Mum really went into one over another newspaper article which claimed that Mum's new single, 'Not Such an Innocent Girl', is 'sugar-coated and overproduced'. Oh dear.

Mum's reaction on these occasions is to go into a terminal sulk. If this keeps up, I may be forced to pitch my *Bob The Builder* play tent in the grounds and camp out until the storm clouds lift.

Monday September 17th

I quite enjoy the change of scene which mornings at nursery school provide, but as I am the only kid whose Mum and Dad are genuine mega-rich Superstars it can be a bit tiresome. Much of this is due to my own celebrity standing, which of course attracts a good deal of attention. The other day one girl offered me 10p if I'd let her kiss me. 'No way, dollface,' I said. 'I get more than that for taking nasty medicine.'

Tuesday September 18th

Mum has finally emerged from her spectacular sulk and this afternoon she was sitting on our Moroccan leather couch watching a wildlife programme on TV. She looked across at Dad, who was reading *The Beano*, and said: 'David, did you know that in Florida they use alligators to make handbags?'

'Really?' said Dad. 'It's amazing what they can train animals to do these days.'

Wednesday September 19th

This morning I discovered a brilliant new word: tantrum. Mum wouldn't let me wear my new Calvin Klein jeans to nursery school, so I threw myself on the floor, went round and round in circles on my back, kicking my heels on the floor and screaming until my face went purple.

'He's throwing a tantrum,' said Mum, when Dad rushed in to see what was happening.

This tantrum thing seems well worth throwing again some time. It may not achieve much (I had to go to school in my scruffy old Paul Smith slacks), but it certainly gets everyone's attention. Eventually, I suppose, it could qualify as an Olympic sport. 'And the next event, ladies and gentlemen, is throwing the tantrum. And first up, for Great Britain, Brooklyn Beckham!'

Thursday September 20th

It's great being out on my own with Dad because he lets me have as many Smarties as I like and in the car he plays records by the divine Britney Spears, as long as I promise not to tell Mum about it. However, shopping with him can be really embarrassing. It's bad enough when he says 'thank you' every time the automatic doors open. But this morning we went into the chemist's for him to buy some deodorant.

'The ball type?' asked the assistant.

'No,' said Dad. 'The kind that goes under your arms.'

And then there was the time we went to the local corner shop for a bottle of sauce.

'HP?' asked the shopkeeper.

'No,' said Dad. 'I'll pay cash.'

Friday September 21st

I'm enjoying life in Hertfordshire but the thing about being in the countryside is that you have to drive everywhere – to nursery school, to the shops, to the West End.

Yesterday Mum and I had a bit of a shouting match. I can't remember what it was about. It was one of those petty things like refusing to let her wash behind my ears or arguing over whether or not she'll buy me a £10,000 Rolex watch like Dad's. Anyway, I threw one of those tantrum things and screamed: 'I hate it here. I'm running away.'

'Wait,' said Mum. 'I'll drive you.'

Saturday September 22nd

But then, parents are funny people anyway. I mean, they make such a big deal of teaching you to walk and talk and then for the rest of your life they keep telling you: 'Sit down and keep quiet.'

Sunday September 23rd

Dad was in a really good mood today and feeling very pleased with himself. He read in the paper that a Chinese restaurant in London has been named after him. It's called Lo Eye Q.

Look, I know it's not funny to keep poking fun at my Dad, but with some of the things he gets up to, you can't help it. Like, when he first left school he went for a job at this big firm in London. They asked him to go outside and fill in a questionnaire, so he went downstairs and punched the doorman.

Monday September 24th

Mum and Dad were on the *Parkinson* TV show with that John Elton and Mum told Parky: 'I think people think I'm a miserable cow in high heels and I just go to Bond Street all the time.' That's not true, of course. Sometimes when she goes to Bond Street she wears low heels.

Why I wasn't also invited on to the show is something of a mystery as I know Parky enjoys grovelling in the company of Superstars and my own unique insights into life at Beckingham Palace would surely have provided fascinating viewing. The fact that filming took place well beyond my bedtime is hardly an excuse for depriving the nation of what would have been a truly enthralling encounter.

On the other hand, Parky probably has it in mind to devote an entire show to me at some later date. Yes, I'm sure that's it.

Tuesday September 25th

Deprived of my own sparkling conversation and wit, Parky was reduced to asking a series of toe-curling personal questions, which elicited the information that Mum's pet name for Dad was 'Goldenballs'. Everyone laughed when she said that but I didn't understand it. Dad keeps all his footballs in the garage and not one of them is golden. Maybe he's got a couple of gold balls he keeps hidden away in case Prince Harry or some other royal kid drops by for a kick-about.

Wednesday September 26th

Mum's got her mouth all twisted up again like a constipated monkey after reading a magazine poll that said she was no longer sexy. I felt for her, but I couldn't help hugging myself because the name at the top of the poll was my own divine, delicious, delectable Britney. I daren't put the article up in my bedroom in case Mum sees it and starts getting jealous, but I'll cut it out and pin it up in one of the rooms that Mum seldom goes into. Like the kitchen.

Thursday September 27th

Drove into London with Dad today and he let me have two whole tubes of Smarties on condition that I didn't tell Mum about the giant packet of Jammie Dodgers he scoffed all by himself on the way in. We went to see Dad's agent and Dad said: 'Tenth floor please' as we got into the lift.

'Uh, there's only eight floors in this building,' said the attendant.

'That's OK,' said Dad. 'Take us up to the eighth and we'll walk the rest.'

Friday September 28th

Poor old Dad. The nearest he'll ever come to a brainstorm is a slight drizzle.

Saturday September 29th

Spurs 3 Manchester United 5

A cracking win, but Spurs went 3–0 up and Dad said that at half time Frosty Fergie gave the Manchester United players one of his shortest ever team talks – which I suppose is easy when you're only using four-letter words. Anyway, it did the trick because the Manchester lads came back like storm-troopers and Dad scored the final goal, which totally silenced the Spurs fans who had been chanting something about Dad wearing Mum's knickers for the entire game. It's always great to stuff one of the London sides, but I only wish it could have been Arsenal rather than Spurs. I've hated those Highbury fans ever since they spotted me in the crowd at one match and started singing an extremely rude version of 'Rock-a-by baby'.

Sunday September 30th

Dad's been included in a list of multi-millionaires who've worked hard for their money. Quite right, too. Running round a football pitch for 90 minutes once a week really takes it out of you.

Not to mention poncing around in Police sunglasses for a measly million a year. And then he has his picture taken a lot, which is quite exhausting, standing under the lights in full make-up. Plus riding around in a limo is very wearying by the end of the day. Oh no, it may look easy, but Dad earns every penny.

OCTOBER
2001

Monday October 1st

After reading a magazine feature that said the Beckhams were 'Superstars Trapped In Their Own Home By Fame', Mum decided that as Besieged Celebrities we should entertain ourselves at home by renting videos. Great, I thought, put me down for *Die Hard* and *Exterminator II*. No such luck. She keeps getting these old black and white movies. Last night it was one called *Guess Who's Coming to Dinner*. They watched it twice, and Dad guessed wrong both times.

Tuesday October 2nd

Mum's been as ill tempered as a giraffe with a sore throat. In the album charts, her new record has been outsold by a *Bob The Builder* CD. Her mood hasn't been improved by me stomping round the house and yelling: 'Can Mum fix it? No she can't!'

I bet they'll cut *that* bit out of the documentary.

Wednesday October 3rd

Dark clouds hover over Beckingham Palace and the long corridors chill with an eerie dampness as one senses that the evil influence of The Big Bad Evil Ginger One is among us again. A celebrity beauty poll has concluded that Mum has the worst complexion in showbiz. And if this alone were not enough to get Mum biting the curtains, the voters agreed that her face is far more blemished than The Evil Ginger One. Mum, of course, begged to differ and suggested that the Ginger Monster looks as though a mortician has gone to work on her and been suddenly called away half way through.

Thursday October 4th

Dad's away with the England team training hard as they prepare to play Greece in another World Cup qualifier. I doubt whether such intense preparations are strictly necessary. It's only Greece, for God's sake. Does the nation that invented football really have anything to fear from a country whose national sport is kebabs?

Friday October 5th

Went with Mum to a store where she was signing copies of *Learning to Fly*. I spilled ice-cream all down the front of my brand-new £50 Burberry shirt and – wouldn't you know it – some prat of a photographer from the *Sun* took a picture of me tearfully surveying the damage. Is there nowhere that Superstars like myself can hide from the harsh glare of fame?

It occurs to me that what I really need is a personal publicist who can shield me from such intrusions. That Max Clifford has rung me several times offering his services, but I must confess I find his clientele a trifle tacky, including as it does high-priced hookers and disgraced cabinet ministers. This is not the kind of company a Superstar chooses to keep and I have something much more upmarket in mind. I've heard that Prince Edward's missus runs a pretty ritzy PR outfit for a small and exclusive group of clients. I must give her a bell some time.

Saturday October 6th

England 2 Greece 2

Engerrland! Engerrland! Dad's a national hero again after scoring an injury-time equaliser against Greece to put England in the World Cup finals. The kebabs played surprisingly well and it looked like England were dead and buried until Captain Marvel stepped up to deliver one of his famous bender free kicks with only seconds to go. It was a real 30-yard curler, more bent than a Mexican traffic cop.

To celebrate, Dad took a big crowd of us out for a curry and I started bawling when I dropped some of my food on the floor. They told me to stop, but I said: 'It's my chapati and I'll cry if I want to.'

Actually, I made that last bit up. But it's good, innit?

Engerrland! Engerrland!

Sunday October 7th

One of the more hysterical reactions to England's win has been the suggestion that Dad should be given a knighthood, seeing as he is being portrayed as a combination of St. George, Winston Churchill and Superman.

Cometh the hour, cometh the man – all that sort of stuff. Mum is quite taken with the idea of becoming Sir Becks and Lady Posh and she has already started doodling a family coat of arms on the back of an envelope.

Monday October 8th

Mum's still working on the coat of arms. So far the best she has come up with is a pair of crossed football boots topped by a golden microphone. Very tasteful.

She has also started to think about what she should wear to the investiture at the Palace and is practising her curtsying in front of the mirror.

Tuesday October 9th

Silent breakfast this morning. Mum's had a face like Columbo's mac ever since Kylie Minogue had the No. 1 song in the Top Ten while Mum's record 'Not Such an Innocent Girl' could only reach No. 6. Things got worse when one of the papers revealed that Dad plays Kylie Minogue records in his car.

'Is that right, David?' snapped Mum.

'Er, yes,' said Dad, adding quickly: 'But I only listen to them with the sound off.'

Wednesday October 10th

An Italian television crew came to the house and inevitably they asked Mum if there was any chance of Dad playing for one of their teams one day. She said it was a possibility, which, knowing Mum, means that she would be off there like a shot if they offered Dad the right kind of wonga. Personally, I doubt that Dad would fancy it. Apart from the language problem, there's the question of food. Seeing Dad eat spaghetti is like watching a kitten unravel a ball of wool. Besides, where can you buy Jammie Dodgers in Milan?

Thursday October 11th

There's no end to the media's fascination with

me and, to a lesser extent, Mum and Dad. A new cable TV show will use *Spitting Image*-type puppets to portray us at home, and the plan is to show Mum and Dad as being a bit thick while featuring me as the brains of the family. So it's another documentary, really.

Friday October 12th

There are all sorts of rumours flying around because Dad has been 'rested' for Manchester United's game with Sunderland tomorrow. Some people seem to think that he has had a bust-up with Frosty Fergie, which wouldn't be difficult. How would you like to work for a man who's a cross between Scrooge and Victor Meldrew? I'd ask Dad about it, but he's flown off to meet Mum who's on a promotional tour in Scandinavia, which just goes to show how desperate she is for publicity now that her solo career seems to be on the skids. I can't imagine the beautiful Britney freezing her lovely ass off in Sweden just to sell a few records.

Saturday October 13th

It's great having the house to myself. For one thing I can play with my train set without Dad leaning over my shoulder shouting: 'Come on, make them crash!' Also I can go into the games room and throw darts at the picture of The Big Bad Evil Ginger One, just like Mum does.

Dad was on the phone from Stockholm today. He wanted to make sure I videoed Friday's episode of *The Tweenies* so that he can watch it when he gets back. I'll check on that once I've finished watching *Sex And The City*.

Sunday October 14th

Mum and Dad are back and I'd have been really pleased to see them except that Mum was so delighted with her Scandinavian trip that she is now going round the house singing along with a CD she brought back. If you think 'Not Such an Innocent Girl' was crap in English, you should hear it in Norwegian.

Monday October 15th

It's well known that Manchester United make a bundle by bringing out new kit so that parents are constantly having to fork out loads of dough for replica shirts and so on. I know it's tough on the working classes, but how else are you going to raise the wages for a Superstar like my Dad? You get what you pay for. The problem is that with all these new strips, Dad often gets confused when he's changing for a match. So now Mum has had each item of kit clearly marked: 'Shirt', 'shorts', 'socks', 'pads'.

Tuesday October 16th

On a German TV chat show Dad insisted that he was 'just a regular bloke'. He'd have sounded a lot more convincing had he not been wearing his regular bloke accessories, including a £50,000 pair of diamond earrings, a £15,000 diamond engagement ring and a custom-made £20,000 diamond watch. Come to think of it, that would be a brilliant name for an upmarket clothing store. Regular Bloke. I like it. They could have one of those snappy slogans. Something like: 'You'll go broke at Regular Bloke – the Store Where Everything Costs More.'

Wednesday October 17th

Being a Regular Bloke, culture is not high on the list of Dad's priorities. His idea of a highbrow evening is a Sylvester Stallone *Rambo* video and a packet of Jammie Dodgers. But that doesn't stop Mum trying to introduce him to some of the finer things in life. Last night she dragged him along to see *Swan Lake* at the Royal Opera House in Covent Garden and Dad couldn't understand why the ballerinas kept standing on their toes.

'Why don't they just get in some taller girls?' he asked.

Thursday October 18th

The media continues to be obsessed with my progress and my lifestyle and increasingly it is me they want to talk about when they interview Mum or Dad. Mum said on a radio phone-in that I was a very privileged child but not spoilt, and explained: 'I don't want a nightmare brat on my hands.' Right on, Ma. But unless I get a miniature Porsche car that I can really drive for my birthday, your nightmares could be just beginning.

Friday October 19th

It's a good job we've got plenty of help in the house, because preparing meals is not Mum's strong point. When she's in the kitchen we can always tell when dinner is ready because the smoke alarm goes off. And if any of her hamburgers are left over, we give them to the cleaning lady to scour the sink with. However, Dad always tries to encourage her.

Last night Mum asked: 'How do you like your potato salad?'

'It's great,' said Dad. 'Tastes just like you bought it yourself.'

Saturday October 20th

Mum's aversion to cooking may well stem from her food fads over the years. She admits in her new book that she once had an eating disorder and at one point ate only packets of peas and steamed vegetables. Big deal. Compared to those jars of spinach and broccoli she used to stuff down me when I was a kid, that was a real gourmet meal. And have you ever seen what that stuff can do to a nappy?

Sunday October 21st

It's been another of those Brooklyn-stop-that-immediately mornings. Mum was in a foul mood because one of the papers had yet another article suggesting that her solo career had taken a nosedive. Me and Dad decided we would be better off elsewhere, so we went for a spin in the Ferrari and it was great until we were stopped by a police car. 'Do you realise you were doing more than 90 miles an hour?' asked the officer.

'I can't have been,' said Dad. 'I've only been out 20 minutes.'

Monday October 22nd

There are new rumours that the Spice Girls have finally disbanded and won't be singing together again. Mind you, getting them to sing together at all was always one of their basic problems.

Tuesday October 23rd

The television crew making the documentary have been laughing all day. They went with Dad when he visited the local surgery for a check-up. When the doctor asked him to strip to the waist, Dad took his trousers off.

Wednesday October 24th

It's official. The Spice Girls really *have* broken up and there is no chance of a reunion. In some quarters this is being hailed as the best news since the eradication of foot-and-mouth disease.

Thursday October 25th

I must say that although the kids in my nursery school are not in the Superstar bracket either financially or celebrity-wise, some of them are quite bright. The other day this cute little blonde called Amy asked me: 'Brooklyn, are you the opposite sex, or am I?' Now that's what I call a good question. An older woman like Phoenix Chi will probably know the answer.

Friday October 26th

I was glad to see that in all the discussion about the Spice Girls breaking up there was no mention of me dumping Baby Spice The Deceiver. Which is just as well. I know The Vultures of Fleet Street are always on the lookout for a juicy scandal and I might have been tempted to give one of the papers a Kiss And Tell story of my relationship with Baby Spice The Deceiver that would make their hair curl, involving, as it does, passion, duplicity, treachery and betrayal.

Saturday October 27th

I can see the headlines now – 'Sizzling Spicy Secrets as Brooklyn Says Bye Bye, Baby'. I am not in the business of peddling sleaze, but I will keep Max Clifford's number handy in case I change my mind.

Sunday October 28th

It goes without saying that a funky kind of guy like me is a big hit with the chicks at nursery school, and I am getting even more attention from them now that word has got out that me and Baby Spice are in Splitsville. The other day a cute little brunette babe called Millie invited me to her birthday party, but Dad said I couldn't go.

'Why not?' asked Mum.

'Well, the invitation says from 4 to 6,' said Dad. 'And Brooklyn's only two.'

Monday October 29th

Experienced in the ways of the world as I am, I must admit that there are times when certain grown-up matters are beyond my grasp. For instance, the *Sun* says that Mum was seen in a Manchester chemist buying a pregnancy test kit. Now, I've heard of football kit or a model aeroplane kit. But a pregnancy test kit? What's that? It's a good job Phoenix Chi is coming round tomorrow. I'll ask her – she's sure to know.

Whatever the answer, the story was of sufficient significance for the *Sun* to put it on the front page. Obviously it is a matter of vital national importance.

Tuesday October 30th

Phoenix Chi: *Yo, Brookie babe. What's happening?*

Brooklyn: *Hi, Chi. Er, what's a pregnancy test kit?*

Phoenix: *Why, my man, that's heavy duty grown-up stuff. Believe me, you don't wanna go there.*

Brooklyn: *My mum's bought one.*

Phoenix: *Whoa, dude, hold it right there! If your momma is messing with that pregnancy test she must think she's gonna have a baby. You could be about to have a little brother, or even a sister.*

Brooklyn: *You mean they make them out of kits?*

Phoenix: *Not exactly, sweet face. Let me explain ...*

Wednesday October 31st

Sorry, dear diary, I am too shocked to write much. The bottom line, as outlined by Phoenix Chi, is that I could be getting a baby brother or, even worse (gulp) a baby *sister*. This calls for emergency measures. I have already hidden my best toys in the innermost depths of the broom cupboard where tiny hands cannot get at them. I must now turn my attention to getting the bedroom door to lock from the inside so that no intruders of the infant variety can cross the threshold. When you're The Most Famous Toddler In Britain you don't relinquish that title without a fight and no new arrival can expect *me* to put out the welcome mat and run the risk of diluting the hard-won approbation of an adoring public. Brooklyn Beckham. That's a brand name. And don't you forget it.

NOVEMBER 2001

Thursday November 1st

I keep checking Mum out but I can't see any sign of that big bump appearing. Maybe she's just holding her stomach in like she does when she has her picture taken. I'll have to catch her in a more relaxed moment.

Friday November 2nd

Mum's still on her culture kick and last night she took Dad to the West End to see that show *Les Miserables*. When they came out, Dad asked: 'Which one was Les?'

Saturday November 3rd

I'm on full scale Baby Alert. Every morning I set my *Bob The Builder* alarm clock so I can creep down the corridor to hear if Mum is being sick in the bathroom, which is something else Phoenix Chi told me about. I am also monitoring the post, keeping an eagle eye out for catalogues from Mothercare.

Sunday November 4th

Some days are just *made* for Superstars and this was one of them. Eat your heart out, kids – I've been to the premiere of the *Harry Potter* film.

Inevitably, the day was not without its drama. To dress for the occasion, I thought something stylish but understated would be in order. Black suit, perhaps, with discreet designer T-shirt. And what does Mum come up with? A loud tartan suit that must have come from a Scottish Oxfam shop. Oh come on, Mum. I'm thinking Armani and you're thinking more like Bozo The Clown. I threw one of those tantrum things, complete with serious heel kicking, but it didn't seem to work. So off I go in the limo looking like a walking crossword puzzle.

As if that wasn't enough, I could hardly hear the movie for some prat called Jonathan Ross who was dressed in a purple suit that made mine look positively tasteful. He kept staring at the screen and saying: 'Cwikey, Bwooklyn, this is bwilliant!' Great. Eight hundred seats in the cinema and they have to put me next to a grown-up who speaks worse than I do.

Monday November 5th

The *Harry Potter* movie is fantastic. It's all about this kid who is a wizard and he has a magic cloak that can make him disappear quicker than one of Mum's records from the Top Ten.

I'm going to have a serious talk with Mum and Dad about getting me into the Hogwarts School of Witchcraft and Wizardry, where Harry Potter goes and where they play a really cool game called Quidditch, which is like mid-air basketball on broomsticks. Sounds much more fun than some place called Eton, where Mum and Dad want me to go when I'm bigger.

Tuesday November 6th

I had hoped to bring up the Hogwarts School of Witchcraft and Wizardry at breakfast this morning, but Mum was busy telling us about this really bad dream she had last night. She was walking down Bond Street, stark naked except for a pair of high-heeled shoes and crowds of people were laughing and pointing at her.

'I could have just died with embarrassment,' she said. 'The shoes were from Marks and Spencer.'

Wednesday November 7th

That's the second strange dream Mum has told us about this week. Maybe it's something to do with this pregnancy lark. I'll ask Phoenix Chi when she comes round tomorrow.

Oh, by the way, I forgot to mention that Harry Potter's sworn enemy is Voldemort, who drinks the blood of unicorns and wants to take over the world. Huh, he doesn't frighten me. When you have been used to going head-to-head with The Big Bad Evil Ginger One, a blood-drinking monster is an absolute pussycat.

Thursday November 8th

Phoenix Chi: *Yo, Brookie baby. Give me some skin. Yeah. What's happening, my man?*

Brooklyn: *Hi, Chi. You remember we spoke about this pregnancy thing?*

Phoenix: *Yeah, dude? You catch anything coming down yet? The bump? The morning sickness?*

Brooklyn: *Not so far. No bump. No sickness.*

Phoenix: *Hmmm. Well, sweetness, you'd better watch what she's eating. Women get these really strange cravings when they're having a baby.*

Brooklyn: *Like what?*

Phoenix: *Well, they start digging all kinds of weird stuff. Like eating pickled onions with Mars bars. Or cauliflower smothered in marmalade.*

Friday November 9th

I can't take my eyes off Mum at meal times. If she starts spreading her toast with Marmite and marshmallows I'll know I'm on to something. I did notice, in passing, that in the morning Dad has taken to drinking a thing called a Prairie Oyster, which is raw eggs mixed with Worcestershire sauce. Maybe he's pregnant, too.

Saturday November 10th

Video night again. This time Mum rented *The Greatest Story Ever Told*.

'What's it about?' asked Dad.

'It's all about God and Jesus and miracles and the Ten Commandments,' said Mum.

'Hmmm,' said Dad. 'I think I'll wait until the book comes out.'

Sunday November 11th

There's rumours flying around that old Frosty Fergie is going to retire as manager of Manchester United at the end of the season. I hope they manage to get someone more cheerful to replace him – he always comes on TV looking like an undertaker at a health farm.

Meanwhile there's still a will-he-won't-he question mark hovering over Dad's new contract at Old Trafford. What the outcome will be only God and Dad's agent knows.

Monday November 12th

Baby Spice The Deceiver has been saying that there's still a possibility the Spice Girls could reunite. If so, it will probably be during the winter months, because I heard Mum say the other evening that it would be a bloody cold day before she got together with that lot again.

Tuesday November 13th

Mum poured orange juice on her cornflakes today. She said it was an accident, but I'm not so sure. Anyway, it's gone down in my Baby Alert book under Strange Eating Habits. No sign of any bump yet, though.

Wednesday November 14th

Mum and Dad got home really late from this very posh dinner at The Savoy last night. They would have been home earlier, but Dad got stuck in the revolving door at the hotel. He couldn't remember whether he was coming out or going in.

Thursday November 15th

What with all the worries about England fans misbehaving, riot police in South Korea are practising for next year's World Cup finals by dressing like soccer hooligans and chanting 'Come On England' and 'David Beckham'. I suspect that when they get around to 'Who ate all the pies?' it might lose a little something in the translation.

It's true, of course, that the behaviour and language of some fans can get a bit out of order. When we go to Old Trafford to watch Dad, Mum tries to cover my ears so I can't hear the chanting. But I've still managed to pick up some brilliant words. I tried out a few of them in nursery school the other day and their reaction was to write Mum a letter and suggest that she come down to the school for an urgent chat. I suppose they want to tell her how well I'm doing.

Friday November 16th

Talking of the World Cup, there was a TV documentary saying that in Korea they eat dogs. Mum says that's probably why The Big Bad Evil Ginger One has always been frightened to go out there. Anyway, it's worth remembering that in Korea, a dog is not just for Christmas. It's for breakfast, lunch and dinner as well.

Saturday November 17th

There's a new mobile phone out which has an 18-carat gold keyboard studded with 1,200 diamonds. It costs £28,000 and Dad is thinking of getting Mum one for Christmas. He says it will be a nice little stocking filler.

Sunday November 18th

The Press never give up, do they? OK, so

they had their fun when Mum dressed me up in that ridiculous checked suit for the *Harry Potter* premiere, but I thought I'd put that particular fashion disaster well behind me. However I had underestimated the depths to which the Vultures of Fleet Street will sink. The comedian Frank Skinner wore a loud check suit on a night out in the West End and one of the papers gleefully pointed out that it was identical to the one I wore to the *Harry Potter* opening. To add to my humiliation, they even reprinted a picture of me in the offending outfit. The only consolation was that this Skinner bloke looked even more of a prat in his than I did in mine. Anyway, the suit is no longer part of my wardrobe. I managed to dump it on our Guy Fawkes bonfire, together with a collection of Winnie the Pooh bibs and a particularly nasty pair of Clark's sandals which I have resolutely refused to wear.

Monday November 19th

Dad's face really lit up when he got home and Mum said: 'Guess what, babes, I've got a marvellous meal planned for you tonight.'

'Really?' said Dad, who sounded surprised.

'Yeah,' said Mum. 'I'll tell you all about it on the way to the restaurant.'

Tuesday November 20th

It continues to dismay me to discover just how much intimate detail of our daily lives at Beckingham Palace Mum is prepared to discuss in public. She told a French TV interviewer that Dad found it more exciting to be in bed with her than to score a goal for England. Exciting? I think not. I sometimes creep into Mum's bed in the morning myself and all she ever says is: 'Go to sleep, Brooklyn, it's too early.'

Wednesday November 21st

Dad's a great one for gadgets, and the bigger and more vulgar they are the better he likes them. His latest acquisition is a new £8,000 fridge-freezer that's so state-of-the-art it's even got a CD player and TV set built in. Now every time mum opens the fridge she pushes the CD button and starts singing along with her single 'Not Such an Innocent Girl'. Is it any wonder that the milk keeps going sour?

Thursday November 22nd

There's lots of posh restaurants within Ferrari-distance of Beckingham Palace, so Mum and Dad took me out to dinner last night and all through the meal Dad kept staring at this bald-headed bloke with glasses because he thought he recognised him from somewhere.

'Maybe he was at school with you,' suggested Mum.

'No,' said Dad. 'We didn't have any bald-headed blokes with glasses in our class.'

Honest, I nearly fell out of my booster seat.

Friday November 23rd

I love my Dad dearly, but there are times when I am forced to question his grip on sanity. This morning, Mum asked: 'David, did you put fresh water in the goldfish bowl?'

'No,' said Dad. 'They haven't drunk what I gave them yesterday yet.'

Saturday November 24th

They say that some people never know when they are well off, and if you are seeking an example of this you need look no further than Baby Spice The Deceiver. She has been moaning that the Spice Girls didn't make as much money as people thought and she hadn't made enough money to retire yet. And whose fault is that, Baby? You could have stuck with me and be set up for life. But no, I wasn't good enough. You'd sooner have some banjo player called Jade. So long, sucker. I'll give you a wave next time I pass the dole queue.

Sunday November 25th

Arsenal 3 Manchester United 1

Dad was hopping mad because the Frenchman who plays in goal for Manchester and clowns around gave away two simple goals. 'That Fabien is a right soppy Barthez,' said Dad. At least, I *think* that's what he said.

Monday November 26th

Some old Australian broad called Germaine Greer says people reckon Dad is a national hero but think Mum is 'just a sabre-toothed, scrawny and grasping' singer who makes drab records, and the best thing she can do is concentrate on having more babies. I wish they wouldn't say these nasty things about my Mum. Vicious words like that are like an arrow through my heart. Especially that bit about having more babies. While on the subject, I have to tell you that my Baby Alert is still on Code Red. However, no sign of a bump yet.

Tuesday November 27th

Now that Frosty Fergie is going, there's a lot of speculation about whether or not Dad will sign a new contract with Manchester United. Personally, I wouldn't mind a move. Maybe to one of the London clubs, like Arsenal, even though I still bear the emotional scars from the humiliating way their fans treated me at Highbury. I mean, Manchester is OK, but it's a bit suburban for a mover and shaker like myself. The more I think about it, the more convinced I become that London is the place to be. Permanently swopping Coronation Street for Bond Street would be no problem.

Wednesday November 28th

Phoenix Chi came by today. She's a girl who

shares my enthusiasm for the delights of the London life.

Phoenix: *Now you're talking, my man. London town, The Smoke — it's where it's all happening. It's made for a groovy dude like yourself.*

Brooklyn: *You think so?*

Phoenix: *Of course, hotlips. I mean, when did you last see a classy chick north of Watford? Half of them up there are still wearing clogs and Gracie Fields headscarves.*

Brooklyn: *So you think there really is a north-south divide?*

Phoenix: *Divide? Different planets, sweetface. For instance, when you're driving up north from London, do you know how you can tell when you are getting close to Manchester?*

Brooklyn: *No. How?*

Phoenix: *The M6 is cobbled.*

Thursday November 29th

You know, there's a lot in what Phoenix Chi says. It really is a different world down south. People actually say 'Hello' instead of 'Ey Oop!' and there is a distinct absence of cloth caps, whippets and racing pigeons. You even get a better class of crime. There's a gang of robbers who hang around the West End in London and follow rich people home to steal their Rolex watches. Up north they're more likely to stake out a Co-op in the hope of nicking a Timex.

Friday November 30th

Yes, a move to Arsenal might be nice. A boy at nursery school says you can get there by tube. Whatever that is. Maybe it's one of those tubes that the newspapers say my Mum's solo career is going down.

DECEMBER 2001

Saturday December 1st

Manchester United 0 Chelsea 3

Hardly a very happy start to the festive season. Manchester in mourning is not a pretty sight. Nor is Frosty Fergie's face, which is so miserable that people are thinking of cancelling Christmas.

Sunday December 2nd

Dad's so humiliated by Saturday's defeat that he's been lying down in a darkened room all day listening to my *Teletubbies* CD. Not even a plate of Jammie Dodgers could tempt him.

Monday December 3rd

Only 21 shopping days to Christmas and Mum took me to this really posh store in the West End where they had a great-looking gadget in the window for £500. Mum asked what it was and the assistant said: 'It doesn't actually do anything. It's just a Christmas present.' So Mum bought five.

Tuesday December 4th

Phoenix Chi came round and we talked about Christmas. 'It's a very caring time of year,' she said. 'If the postmen find a package marked "fragile" they only throw it underarm.'

Wednesday December 5th

As winter tightens its grip I regret to report that my Dad has adopted the poncy Continental habit of wearing gloves on the pitch when it gets chilly. Last weekend he came on wearing just one glove, like Michael

Jackson. Dad said this was because the weather forecast had said that on the one hand it could get cold but on the other hand it might stay warm.

Thursday December 6th

I'm not sure Dad can be trusted when it comes to Christmas presents. Mum says she rather fancies something small, sexy and expensive in silk, so Dad's asked Frankie Dettori the jockey to come round on Christmas morning.

Friday December 7th

Panic. In the move to Beckingham Palace, Mum and Dad have mislaid their Christmas card list. Now they have no idea who their friends are.

Monday December 10th

Mum still insists on getting these boring old films on video. Last night she was about to watch one called *Moby Dick* when Dad got really angry and said: 'Fancy renting a sex film. Have you forgotten we've got a child in the house?'

'It's not a porno film,' said Mum. 'It's about whales.'

'That's even worse,' said Dad. 'I can't stand the Welsh.'

Tuesday December 11th

Choosing a Christmas present for Dad is proving difficult. Mum said this morning: 'David, now that we have all this money, I was thinking of getting you a Renoir for Christmas.'

'That's a lovely thought, dollface,' said Dad. 'But don't we already have enough cars?'

Wednesday December 12th

Dad was voted BBC Sports Personality of the Year and he was close to tears when they made the award. It was quite touching. The only other time I've seen him cry was when I stepped on a little engine he'd made all by himself out of Lego.

Thursday December 13th

Dear Father Christmas,

As you have so far failed to respond to any of my faxes and emails I thought I would send you my Christmas list through the post:

1. *Super blow-up picture of Britney Spears in schoolgirl uniform.*
2. *Harry Potter magic cloak.*
3. *Nimbus Two Thousand Harry Potter broomstick.*
4. *Harry Potter spectacles.*
5. *Robot Wars: Advanced Destruction video game.*
6. *Wipeout Fusion racing game.*
7. *Swiss Army penknife (super deluxe*

version with 374 attachments).

8. Twenty-three-foot python in cage (*I saw one in a zoo once and it was brilliant*).

9. Chemistry set with stink bomb capability.

NOT WANTED:

1. Clark's sandals and Winnie the Pooh bibs.

2. Baby sister.

3. Baby brother.

Friday December 14th

The papers are saying Dad is 'spitting blood' after a row with Frosty Fergie. Well, I've been all over the house, including the bathrooms, and I can't find any blood anywhere. Maybe he just spits it into his handkerchief.

Saturday December 15th

Mum gave me a big hug today and said that I was going to get a 'really big surprise' at

Christmas. That can only mean one thing. The Blasted Baby. Maybe it's arrived already. I searched the closets, and cupboards and several secret hiding places Mum thinks I don't know about and while I came across some interesting-looking Christmas parcels with my name on them there was no sign of a baby. If she is keeping the kid somewhere in the house, she's made a good job of it.

Sunday December 16th

Mind you, I haven't searched the grounds. It could be in the gardener's shed or the swimming pool hut. I'll get out my *Bob The Builder* bike with the training wheels and have a look round tomorrow.

Monday December 17th

Not a sniff of a baby anywhere. Maybe they'll get Harrods to deliver it on Christmas Eve with the rest of the stuff.

Tuesday December 18th

Christmas sends Mum into a shopping frenzy and she has been doing some serious damage to our American Express Platinum-Plus VIP card. After several trips up the West End with Mum, Dad says he is sick and tired of shopping. He thinks they should hold Christmas earlier in the year, when the stores are less crowded.

Wednesday December 19th

The papers are saying that Manchester United are ready to ditch Dad if they can't agree on a new contract. Maybe that's Mum's Christmas surprise – we're moving on. I certainly hope so. I'd rather have a new club than a new baby.

Thursday December 20th

The postman delivered a big box and I thought at first it might be the new baby. But it turned out to be an illuminated tableau of the Twelve Days of Christmas, which is now strung across the front of the house, next to the blow-up Santa Claus and the giant banner which says 'Christmas Greetings From The Manchester United Supporters Club (Sawbridgeworth Branch)'.

A thought has just struck me. If this baby is going to be such a big surprise, maybe Mum's getting Father Christmas to deliver it with the rest of the goodies. Methinks urgent action is called for.

Friday December 21st

Dear Father Christmas,

If you have a new baby addressed to Beckingham Palace, Hertfordshire, please do not put it on your sleigh with the rest of the toys as it is a mistake. We already have one baby which is me (although I am a big boy now). If you have this other baby, please give it away

to someone who needs it as it is surplus
to requirements around here.
Merry Christmas
Brooklyn Beckham
PS On Christmas Eve I normally go to
sleep about 7 o'clock.

Saturday December 22nd

Mum was going round the house singing 'Once In Royal David's City'. It sounded awful, but I think it's nice that someone wrote a Christmas carol about Dad.

Sunday December 23rd

Only two days to go. Hope Santa got my second note about the baby. You can't trust the mail this time of year.

Monday December 24th

I've set the alarm for 5 o'clock. If there's a new baby under the tree in the morning, emergency measures may be called for before anyone else wakes up. I've already established that there is plenty of room in the rubbish bin. I did think of dumping it in the garage, but it's full of unworn designer freebies.

Tuesday December 25th

Christmas morning was brilliant. Dad surprised Mum with a fur coat. She'd never seen him in one before. And no sign of a new baby anywhere! Mum's big secret was that she had invited Phoenix Chi and her Mum for Christmas dinner and we all had a great time pulling Christmas crackers even if Dad didn't understand the jokes inside them.

Q. *'What happened to the man who jumped off a bridge in Paris?'*
A. *'He went in Seine.'*

Boom boom!

Wednesday December 26th

I got some really neat presents including a

complete Harry Potter outfit. I'm not sure that it's working properly, however, as I can't fly yet but I suppose I'll have to read the instructions again.

Thursday December 27th

My other favourite present was an Action Man set, complete with combat uniform, rocket launcher, flamethrower, M16 rifle, machine gun and hand grenades. It came in wrapping paper marked: Peace On Earth.

Friday December 28th

Mum was thrilled with the expensive new watch Dad got her for Christmas. Ask her the time and she says: 'It's 2 rubies past 4 diamonds.'

Saturday December 29th

Phoenix Chi got me this brilliant Britney Spears album and I've been playing it in my room because Mum makes this funny face whenever I put it on downstairs. Oh Britney baby, we may be separated by an ocean but my heart is right there by your side. Let's make 2002 our special year, the year we get it on. Brooklyn and Britney. B and B. See what I mean? We belong together, like bed and breakfast.

Sunday December 30th

Dad skinned his knees falling off the rollerblades he was given for Christmas. But Mum put one of my special Mickey Mouse ouchless plasters on the grazes and he stopped sobbing when she let him have a whole packet of jelly babies all to himself.

Monday December 31st

Well, goodbye 2001 and what a year it's been! New house, new love, new horizons. And no new baby. How sweet it is.

JANUARY 2002

Tuesday January 1st

Dad kept all the jokes from the Christmas crackers and he's still going through them, trying to work them out.

Q. *What's the best place to go when you're dying?*
A. *The living room.*

Yes, folks, every one a winner!

Wednesday January 2nd

Me and Mum opened the Harrods sale in London, riding in a carriage with the store owner, Mohamed Al Fayed. Funny bloke, that Mohamed. When we left, he handed me a brown envelope and asked if I could help him to get a British passport.

Thursday January 3rd

New Year's resolutions:

1. *Learn to fly like Harry Potter (this is proving more difficult than I thought, even with the aid of the Nimbus Two Thousand broomstick which yesterday badly let me down in midair as I attempted to fly from my bed to the bean bag in the corner).*
2. *Use my magic Harry Potter powers to rid Mum forever of the curse of The Big Bad Evil Ginger One.*

3. Marry Britney Spears.

4. Persuade Mum to take singing lessons.

5. Get Dad to stop making noises like a racing car with his mouth when he's driving the Ferrari.

Friday January 4th

Dad had to go up to Manchester and when he got back he looked really sick. He said it was because he had to make the whole journey home with his back to the engine, which he hates.

'Why didn't you ask the person opposite to swop seats?' asked Mum.

'I couldn't,' said Dad. 'There was no one sitting there.'

Saturday January 5th

Oh, oh, here we go again. The papers are speculating that Dad might be off to play for Barcelona or Real Madrid. But I don't need to remind you how difficult the language problem would be if we lived abroad. Dad thinks 'manual labour' is a Spanish trade union official.

Sunday January 6th

I've just had a brilliant idea. Dad could go to play for one of those American soccer clubs, like the Tampa Bay Rowdies. That way I would be closer to the beautiful Britney and could spend more time convincing her once and for all that Justin Timberhead just isn't the one for her. This long-distance courtship is tearing me apart and I know how poor Britney must be feeling, having no contact with me other than the occasional letter. Life would be sublime if we could get it together in the good old U.S. of A.

Monday January 7th

Just when 2002 was looking good, the peace and tranquillity of Beckingham Palace is shattered by the sound me and my new teddy bear have come to dread. Even as we speak I am covering teddy's ears. Mum spends all day singing her new single, 'A Mind Of Its Own'. Pity she hasn't got a voice of her own to go with it.

Tuesday January 8th

Mum says the record is being released next month. So it should be, poor things, to put it out of its misery.

Wednesday January 9th

The more I think about Dad going to play in the United States, the more I like the idea. After all, given that I was conceived in Brooklyn that practically makes me an American citizen already.

Thursday January 10th

Dad has been going round the house all day giggling to himself. He finally got one of the Christmas cracker jokes.

Q. *What pantomime is set in a chemist's shop?*

A. *Puss in Boots.*

I like that one, too.

Friday January 11th

I've called off the Baby Alert. Mum's showing no sign of a bump and when I listen at the bathroom door all I can hear is mum singing her new single. Come to think of it, the sound of her being sick might be preferable. Anyway, she obviously thinks this new record is her way back into the Big Time and I hardly think she'd want the comeback hindered by the arrival of a scrawny, howling brat. Changing nappies in between recording sessions at the Abbey Road Studios would be decidedly uncool.

Saturday January 12th

Phoenix Chi says that whole baby thing must

have been a false alarm, whatever that means. Is there a bell that rings when a baby is on the way? Anyway, Phoenix Chi reckons I can relax, there obviously isn't going to be a Blasted Baby, which is a big relief.

Sunday January 13th

Now I know that there is going to be no baby to threaten the status of The Most Famous Toddler in Britain, I have rescued my best toys from the broom cupboard and restored them to the nursery. I'm sleeping better at night, too. I was having nightmares about sharing.

Monday January 14th

I don't know where we'd live if we went to America. California, I guess. That would be the natural home for a groovy, laid back guy like me.

Tuesday January 15th

California dreamin,' on such a winter's day ...

Wednesday January 16th

A beach house in Malibu, perhaps. Yeah, I can just see it now, me and Britney strolling hand-in-hand on the beach, soaking up a few rays. Driving in my Corvette up the Pacific Coast Highway with the top down. Larging it up on Sunset Boulevard. Hooray for Hollywood!

Thursday January 17th

Dad's finally getting the hang of the computer he had for Christmas and he's getting on fine now that Mum has wiped all the white marks off the screen and explained that you don't need to use Tipp-Ex to correct your mistakes.

Friday January 18th

Blimey, he is getting keen! 'There's this really useful book all about words which someone told me about and I want to order on the

Internet,' he said. 'How do you spell dikshunry?'

Saturday January 19th
Manchester United 2 Blackburn Rovers 1

Mum and Dad took me to Old Trafford and I overheard old Frosty Fergie giving his team talk before the match. He told them: 'Now lads, as you know, this game is all about self-reliance, self-discipline, leadership, responsibility and individualism. So go out there and play exactly as I've told you to.'

Incidentally, it looks as though old Frosty Fergie won't be retiring after all. We've got to put up with that miserable face for another season or two. I didn't see him crack a smile all over Christmas and when he called by with some presents the garden gnomes ran and hid.

Sunday January 20th
Dad is still telling the knock-knock jokes we got out of the Christmas crackers.

Knock knock!
Who's there?
Mandy.
Mandy who?
Mandy lifeboats.

Monday January 21st

They get worse.

Knock knock!
Who's there?
Harry.
Harry who?
Harry up, it's cold out here.

No more, I promise.

Tuesday January 22nd

Manchester United 0 Liverpool 1

Dad was in a foul mood and said the referee
was an absolute banker. At least, I think that's
what he said. But why on earth would they

have a bloke from NatWest refereeing a football match?

Wednesday January 23rd

Contract negotiations with Manchester United continue, but I don't know why Dad bothers. America is definitely where we should be.

Thursday January 24th

It's amazing how people can go through life existing on a delusion. Take Mum, for instance. She has just been on *GMTV* and boasted that her music is 'bloody good'. Yeah, Mum. And it's even bloody better when it stops.

Friday January 25th

Which reminds me. Mum has made a French language version of her latest single, 'Mind Of Its Own'. I think it's a very good idea. After all, now we're part of the EEC it's only fair that all we Europeans should be made to suffer together.

Saturday January 26th

I think I'll send a letter to the beautiful Britney, telling her of my plans for America. She hasn't actually replied to any of my letters yet, but I'll continue to post them up the chimney just like you do when you write to Santa.

My darling Britney,

I haven't received a reply to my letters yet, but I am not really surprised as there is an awful lot of thieving in the Post Office over the Christmas period. I just thought I would let you know that there is a strong possibility that I am coming to live in America, which means I will be very near you. I could take you out for a Happy Meal at the McDonalds in Malibu and you could have both of the free toys that come with it (I believe that at the moment they are doing a very nice line in Harry Potter merchandise). Talking of Harry Potter, I had one of his magic broomsticks for Christmas and I am hoping to fly over to see you soon. Don't worry if you can't see me, as I will probably be wearing my Harry Potter cloak and it makes me invisible.

Lost of love,

Brooklyn Beckham.

Sunday January 27th

I look out of the window and it's nothing but grey skies and rain. I can't wait to get to that California sunshine.

Monday January 28th

Just in case I forget, I've started making a list of things I want for my birthday;

1. *Map of film stars' homes in Hollywood.*
2. *Beach Boys CD.*
3. *Surf board.*
4. *Los Angeles Dodgers baseball cap.*
5. *Corvette convertible (preferably bright red).*

Tuesday January 29th

I think Mum would like it in America. They say there's some really serious shopping to be done on that Rodeo Drive in Beverly Hills. The place is full of those boutiques that she likes. You know, the ones with just a couple of cashmere jumpers and an artfully draped silk scarf in the window and no price tags so that right up until the last moment you can retain the excitement of not knowing exactly how much you are being ripped off for.

Wednesday January 30th

Maybe we could live next door to some famous film star, like Buzz Lightyear or

Mickey Mouse. And if I got lost, that dog called Lassie could come and find me, just like on TV, especially if I fell down a well and nobody knew where I was and the dog could bark and people would tell him to keep quiet but he would keep on barking and then someone would say 'wait, I think he's trying to tell us something' and then they would follow him and I would be found and everybody would pat Lassie and they would give him a bone because he's a good dog.

Thursday January 31st

California dreamin' is one thing, but in the meantime, beneath the wintry skies of Hertfordshire, I continue to live with the routine of reality, which in our house can lead you down some strange by-ways. This morning I went into the bathroom to find Dad jumping up and down on the spot. 'I just took my cough medicine,' he explained, 'and I forgot to shake the bottle.'

FEBRUARY
2002

Friday February 1st

Mum was in a really foul mood, moaning about her and Dad not being able to go out and about like they used to now we are Superstars Trapped In Our Own Home By Fame. 'Sod it!' she said. 'Why don't we just give the bodyguards the night off and go out clubbing like we used to and get hammered on vodka and Red Bull.'

'Great idea,' said Dad. 'If you get home before me, don't forget to leave the hall light on.'

Saturday February 2nd

No more California dreamin'. I asked Mum straight out about going to America and she said we couldn't even think about moving abroad at the moment because she had other more important things on her mind. What can she mean?

Sunday February 3rd

My darling Britney,

Just when I lived in hope that we could be together, it seems that we are doomed to stay oceans apart. But our love will be a bridge to each other's hearts.

Yours eternally,
Brooklyn Beckham.

Monday February 4th

Fear and apprehension stalk the hairdressers of the land. Dad has begun to grow his hair on top and at the back and there are signs that he is planning to bring back the dreaded mullet style, as sported by footballers like Chris Waddle and Glen Hoddle in the 1980s.

Tuesday February 5th

Who knows what other fashions disaster might be revived if the mullet makes a comeback. Flared trousers, medallions?

Wednesday February 6th

Mum is constantly nagging Dad about how he is too modest and refuses to demand the respect his celebrity status deserves. One of her pet moans is about the figure 7 which he wears on his Manchester United shirt. She thinks that now he is a Superstar he should have an unlisted number.

Meanwhile, Dad has been talking publicly about his relationship with Manchester United. He says he looks upon the club as his extended family. Now, just hold on a minute, pops. If this means I have to start called old Frosty Fergie 'uncle', you can forget it.

Thursday February 7th

Dad still hasn't signed his new contract with Manchester United. The question of holidays is the main stumbling block. Mum has told Dad to ask for every Saturday afternoon off so they can go shopping.

Friday February 8th

I threw one of those tantrum things again today because Mum had failed to recharge the battery on my mobile phone, so I got sent to my room, which is pretty heavy-duty punishment when you think that all I have up there is half of Hamley's toy store, state-of-the-art satellite TV with 54 channels and

£30,000 worth of Hi-fi equipment. But as I lay there watching *The Simpsons*, I couldn't help thinking: Mum and Dad seem to consider themselves indispensable, but I'm not so sure. I mean, Santa Claus brings us presents, Fortnum and Mason deliver our food, midwives deliver babies, policemen protect us and firemen put out fires. Who needs parents?

Saturday February 9th

Funny how you can lie there thinking of silly little things when you're bored. For instance, before Dad met Mum, I wonder who told him how to drive?

Sunday February 10th

Something's going on. Mum and Dad have started talking in some kind of code, spelling out certain words so I can't understand what they're saying. They could just be planning a surprise birthday party for me, but I think there's more to it than that. The thing is, they can be talking quite normally and the moment I walk into the room they start the spelling bit.

Monday February 11th

They're at it again, spelling out words and then looking at me and smiling and then cuddling each other a lot. There's definitely something dodgy afoot. I think I'll run it by Phoenix Chi.

Tuesday February 12th

I swear that Mum only just about stopped herself from kicking the cat today. And all because the papers are saying that Virgin records are going to dump her because she's past her sell-by date and her solo career has turned out to be a real bummer as far as record sales are concerned, which is all a pack of lies. Oops, she's just thrown a jar of sundried tomatoes at the kitchen wall. Now, now, mummy. Temper, temper!

Wednesday February 13th

Cripes, I think they might be right! Dad's hair is definitely on the brink of giving birth to a mullet. Come to think of it, I haven't had my own hair cut for a few weeks now. Yipes! I hope they're not grooming me for a mullet, too. I'd be the laughing stock of the nursery school. Dad, don't do this to me, please.

Thursday February 14th

There's talk about Dad being given a walk-on part in Coronation Street. If so, I hope he gets the chance to give that Fred Elliott the butcher a kick up the backside. I say I hope he gets the chance to give that Fred Elliott the butcher a kick up the backside.

Friday February 15th

You see, this Fred Elliott bloke always says everything twice. I say this Fred Elliott bloke always says everything twice. Yes, it annoys the hell out of me, too.

Saturday February 16th

Phoenix Chi came round and, boy, was I glad to see her.

Phoenix: *Yo, Brookie baby. What's going down?*

Brooklyn: *I wish I knew. There's definitely something Mum and Dad don't want me to hear. They keep spelling words out.*

Phoenix: *What kind of words, sweetface?*

Brooklyn: *Well, I first noticed it when she looked at Dad and said: 'David, I think I may be ... ' and then spelled out something and they hugged each other.*

Phoenix: *So what do you think she was saying?*

Brooklyn: *I dunno. First of all I thought she could be saying, 'David, I think I* may be No. 1 in the charts.' But I know that's impossible.

Phoenix: *Oh, you are such a dumb dude. The word, my man, is pregnant. Your momma is having a baby. You don't need to be 007 to crack that code!*

Sunday February 17th

It's all coming clear to me now. Once you use 'pregnant' as a key word, everything else falls into place. The conversations keep coming back to me and once you fill in the blanks it all becomes chillingly obvious. 'What would you prefer, David, a *spellitout* or a *spellitout*?' See what I mean? A boy or a girl?

And they're using other codes to keep me in the dark, too. Like: 'When do you think we should tell You-Know-Who that I'm You-Know-What?'

Monday February 18th

Now let's not get too panicky over this.

You're nearly three years old, so let's face this in a grown-up way. It could be another of those false alarms, although I haven't heard any bells going off.

Tuesday February 19th

That's the trouble with Phoenix Chi. She's always jumping to conclusions. Particularly if it's anything to do with sex, and in her book everything is to do with sex.

Wednesday February 20th

Like, where's the evidence? Where's the bump? The morning sickness? The craving for peanut butter and fish-paste sandwiches?

Thursday February 21st

I mean, all that thing with the pregnancy test kit came to nothing just before Christmas. So let's not jump the gun here, Chi baby. Let's not meet disaster half way.

Talking of disasters, there are rumours that

Virgin are dumping Mum because her solo CD's have been about as popular as woodworm in a cripple's crutch, which isn't true. At least I hope it isn't true. They say hell hath no fury like a woman scorned. Oh no? Just imagine a Spice Girl with no recording contract.

Friday February 22nd

Please excuse the shaky writing, dear diary, but I have just received some shattering news. It's true. Mum really IS having another baby. She put out a Press release and also pinned up a notice on the gates of Beckingham Palace, just like the royals do. Jenny Bond will be turning up on the doorstep any time now.

Apart from the unthinkable short-term prospect of having to share my toys, this turn of events could have serious repercussions on my future as The Most Famous Toddler in Britain. Put it in the plural and it dilutes the distinction in a most unacceptable and alarming manner. I do not relish the idea of being referred to in picture captions as Brooklyn Beckham (left).

I can write no more. I'm going to my room to lie down and listen to my *Bob The Builder* CD while the full impact of this momentous development sinks in. I will also have to seriously consider my options as far as the future is concerned. At this precise moment, emigrating to Nepal is emerging as the most likely solution.

Saturday February 23rd

Mum keeps grabbing me by both cheeks, shaking my head from side to side and telling me over and over again that I'm going to have a little brother or a little sister. I don't *want* a baby brother or sister. I'd sooner have a mountain bike.

The thing is, I wasn't consulted about this. I mean, did they deign to elicit my opinion before they placed their order for this Blasted

Baby which threatens to totally disrupt the Beckham household as we know it? Did they hell! So it's no good grabbing me by the cheek and expecting me to join in the jollity. My life as The Most Famous Toddler in Britain is over, my singular celebrity status destroyed at a stroke. And my guitar gently weeps.

Sunday February 24th

The papers are in a feeding frenzy over what the Blasted Baby will be called. As you know, I was called Brooklyn because that's the New York area where I was conceived (I learned all about that conceiving stuff from Phoenix Chi). There is speculation that it could be called anything from Harlow to Old Trafford. On reflection, however, I reckon Mum and Dad got together on this one a month or so back when they suddenly came over all lovey-dovey one chilly afternoon and disappeared into the summer house at the end of the garden, refusing to come out even when I risked serious damage to my favourite Adidas trainers by kicking the door. If I'm right, I'm beginning to feel slightly sorry for this new kid. Fancy going through life with a name like Gazebo.

Monday February 25th

William Hill are offering all kinds of bets on the new arrival, including odds of 100–1 that he'll be a boy and grow up to play football for England. My worst fears are being realised. The Blasted Baby's not even born and it's already being treated like some kind of celebrity.

Tuesday February 26th

This is getting ridiculous. Now you can even bet on the colour of the kid's eyes or what weight it will be.

Wednesday February 27th

The only bet I'm making is that this Blasted Baby won't get anywhere near all that good stuff in my bedroom. If this new kid wants toys, let it comb through the Harrods catalogue like I had to. It might as well learn from the beginning how tough life can be.

Thursday February 28th

At last, some good news to take me away from the insanity of this baby business. All those letters I posted up the chimney have finally paid off. The beautiful Britney is coming to Britain in a few weeks' time. She's obviously coming to see me but, in order to afford us a little privacy from the prying lenses of The Vultures of Fleet Street she has invented this cunning cover story about being in London for the premiere of her new film. Oh Britney baby, my heart is on hold ...

MARCH
2002

Friday March 1st

Dad's not too impressed by the news that the England team are taking supplies of Jaffa Cakes to Japan to boost their energy in the World Cup. So he's sticking to his original plan of taking a spare suitcase full of Jammie Dodgers.

Saturday March 2nd

I continue to learn what it must be like to live in an institution for the insane. This morning I caught Dad standing in front of the mirror with his eyes closed. He said he was trying to see what he looked like while he was asleep.

Sunday March 3rd

My third birthday tomorrow. I've invited the beautiful Britney, but no reply so far. Maybe she's going to surprise me and come bursting out of the cake. Wow, three years old. I look around at those framed pictures of me as a baby, dribbling jars of Heinz baby food down my bib, and I can't believe it was really all those years ago that I was born into Superstardom. Where does the time go?

Monday March 4th

Well, as birthday gigs go, this one was pretty low-key, particularly when you consider my Superstar status. Mum and Dad paid £3,000 to hire a Manchester cinema so me and some other footballers' kids could watch *Monsters Inc.* without having to rub shoulders with anyone whose Dad wasn't famous. Then we had a party with clowns and face painting and all that stuff and a cake in the Manchester United colours (much to my disappointment, Britney didn't come jumping out of it). All very nice, but personally I'd have settled for a few bottles of bubbly at the Groucho Club and a plate of Eggs Benedict at The Ivy. Such a mature celebration would surely be more appropriate for someone who is on the threshold of being able to put his shoes on by himself.

An amusing diversion was supplied by the sight of two of Dad's Manchester United teammates having their top-of-the-range cars towed away from outside the cinema. They explained that they hadn't put any coins in the parking meters because anything to do with money is normally left to their agents.

Tuesday March 5th

Thoughts on being three. These are the things I'm glad to be leaving behind me:

NAPPIES: *Wearing them was like walking around with a bag of wet cement strapped to your bum. Besides, they ruined the line of my designer jeans.*

POTTY TRAINING: *Sitting with your trousers round your ankles watching* Teletubbies *while listening to a chorus of voices urging 'Brooklyn do poos' was not my idea of fun.*

JARS OF BABY FOOD: *Yuk! They taste like Dale Winton speaks.*

BABY TALK: *No more Gucci-Gucci-goo from Mum, thank goodness. Why can't grown-ups talk to babies without thrusting their faces within 2 inches of yours? I've inhaled enough cheap aftershave, dodgy perfume, bad breath and cigarette fumes to fuel a worldwide outbreak of gas warfare.*

Wednesday March 6th

I'm becoming quite a party animal. Today it

was off to London in the limo to see Bob The Builder's new stage show. Could he fix it? Yes he could. Pity he couldn't have fixed the guest list, though. I was the only genuine celebrity there. The rest were decidedly B-list brats, belonging to minor Mums and Dads from *EastEnders*, breakfast television and Page Three girls. I can only assume that Max Clifford sent out the invitations. Phoenix Chi was there and we exchanged High Fives, but the formerly fragrant Baby Spice just threw me a lingering glance across a crowded room. Your loss, baby.

Meanwhile, the beautiful Britney has a really wicked new record out called 'I'm Not A Girl, Not Yet A Woman'. I know how you feel, babe – I'm not a girl, either. Or a woman, come to think of it. Hey! We gotta lot in common …

Thursday March 7th

Oh the shame, the ignomy, the sheer

wretchedness. Dad has signed up to develop a line of boys' clothing. And for whom? You may well ask. Armani, perhaps? Or Ralph Lauren? Hugo Boss? Not at all. It's for – aaargh! I can't say it. OK. Calm down. Let's be grown up about this. It's for (gulp) Marks and Spencer! Hey, this is one modelling gig you definitely *don't* drag me into, Daddy-O. Dolce and Gabbana? Maybe. But Marks and Spencer? In your dreams!

Friday March 8th

The irony is that this Marks and Spencer thing should come along just as Dad is voted Britain's most stylish man by *GQ* magazine. They put *me* at No. 17, which is a bit of a bummer. However I draw some comfort from the fact that Jonathan Ross, the prat in the purple suit who sat next to me at the *Harry Potter* premiere, was voted Britain's worst-dressed. Never was an accolade so wichly deserved. Weally.

Saturday March 9th

I think Mum and Dad have sensed how insecure I'm feeling about this new baby because the *Sun* says they are spending £10,000 on a 20-ft bronze statue of me that will stand in the grounds of Beckingham Palace. I'd have felt even more secure if it was made of gold, but still, it's a nice gesture.

Phoenix Chi came round and she was fuming about the *Bob The Builder* show. 'The whole thing was so *yesterday*, an out-of-date parody of working-class life based on institutionalised prejudices and preconceived stereotyping,' she moaned. 'And sexist, too. Instead of *Bob The Builder*, why couldn't they do a show about a more modern and inspirational role model such as Suzy The Social Worker or Sally The Stress Counsellor?'

Phew. Sometimes that Phoenix Chi can be really weird.

Sunday March 10th

Yipes! Mum has told a newspaper that she wants 'four or five children'. Well, if they expect me to shift over to make room for them in the limo, they've got another think coming.

The TV documentary on Mum, *Being Victoria Beckham*, which I told you about, has just been shown. Mum recalled the time when there was a threat to kidnap me and said: 'Brooklyn lived like a prisoner. It was awful.' I'll say it was. To take my mind off things, Mum used to sing me to sleep every night, an excruciating experience which tempted me to phone the kidnappers and tell them where I was.

Some idea of the general level which the documentary struck can be gleaned from this snippet in which Mum and Dad delivered a revealing insight into the rich and exciting lives they lead:

Dad: *Last night we watched* What Lies Beneath.

Mum: *Scary film. We wanted to go to the toilet, but we couldn't because we was so scared. We was so scared, wasn't we?*

Dad: *We was.*

Riveting stuff, I think you'll agree.

Monday March 11th

Gloom and misery at Beckingham Palace. One of our dogs has gone missing. Mum phoned Dad to tell him the bad news and said: 'I don't know what I'll do without that dog, David. We were so close, I could swear that at times he was actually talking to me.'

'Better hang up, then,' said Dad. 'He might be trying to get through right now.'

Tuesday March 12th

Now that Mum is definitely having a second baby, Dad is getting dead worried about her having any more. He read somewhere that every third child born in the world is Chinese.

Wednesday March 13th

Forgive my slightly sardonic smile, dear diary, but I am relishing the news that Baby Spice The Deceiver has split with her boy friend Jade Jones. So Jade wasn't so precious after all, eh Baby? Heh, heh. Well, don't come running back to me on the rebound. I am Britney's now and there is no turning back.

Thursday March 14th

There's going to be a statue of Dad in Madame Tussaud's and everyone is making cracks about him joining the other dummies, which I feel is a touch unkind.

So far there has been no mention of my good self joining Dad in the Tussaud's line-up but it can only be a matter of time before they spot this obvious gap in their array of celebrities. Which poses the problem of what my wax effigy should wear. Something by Armani, perhaps, or a pair of Bill Blass slacks with a cashmere sweater slung casually over one shoulder. Now, if I only had my own personal stylist (a necessity which I have been trying to impress upon Mum for some time now) I would not be in such a quandary.

Friday March 15th

Anyway, my own image has already been preserved for posterity, by an artist who has portrayed me as a Hindu God in full Manchester United kit. I must confess it is somewhat startling to be given God-like status but then, given my meteoric ascendance to Superstardom, I suppose it was inevitable.

Saturday March 16th

West Ham 3 Manchester United 5

Dad scored twice, confirming that the kick-abouts against me and the garden gnomes have sharpened his game. If he can keep up this form for the World Cup, England will walk it. I have put the gnomes on standby as possible substitutes.

Sunday March 17th

Talking of the World Cup, Mum and Dad have decided to throw a party to give England a good send-off. Nothing elaborate, just a cosy little get-together in the back garden costing no more than half a million pounds. The whole England team will be there, plus what the papers refer to as a star-studded guest list, although, glancing down these names, I am not entirely convinced of their stellar quality. Who, for instance, is Graham Norton? Also, they had left out the beautiful Britney, so I have written her name in at the top. Lucky for me Dad had written the whole thing in crayon, so they won't notice this sly insertion.

Monday March 18th

If anyone spotted a strange object in the sky over Hertfordshire today, it was probably my heart, soaring like an eagle in full flight. The beautiful Britney has split with her boyfriend, Justin Timberhead, and is a free woman. In a week she will be in London. I count the hours on my *Bob The Builder* watch.

Tuesday March 19th

Watching the divine Britney on TV and listening to her silken voice, I feel that I know her already. However, I've been wondering how to greet this wondrous creature when I meet her for the first time in the flesh (and, oh, what flesh it is). Something cool and casual, perhaps. 'Hi, Brit baby. What's happenin'?' Or maybe something more passionate, more *Pride and Prejudice*. You know: 'Oh Britney, my love. My agony is at last ended as I gaze for the first time upon your fair countenance. I tremble at your touch, your merest glance is the torch that lights the burning hunger inside me.' I'll have to think about it.

Wednesday March 20th

On reflection, I think I'll opt for the Darcy approach. These American chicks really dig that classy English stuff.

Thursday March 21st

The bookies are offering odds of 25–1 on Mum giving birth to more than one baby, which is something I've never even considered. Twins or even (gulp) triplets don't even bear thinking about. How could we all fit in the back of the Ferrari?

Also, you could imagine the Press feeding-frenzy if it actually was triplets? *Hello!* magazine would be clearing the decks for a special edition and the Beckham Babes would be the most sought-after infants in the world.

And where would this leave me, The Most Famous Toddler in Britain? Eclipsed. A back number. Mr. Yesterday's man.

Our Father, which art in heaven, please don't let it be triplets.

Friday March 22nd

It's not often that Mum and Dad have an argument (they are, after all, Britain's Most Loving Couple). However, they had a humdinger last night. 'All right,' screamed Mum, 'so I spend a lot of money. Name one other extravagance I have!'

Saturday March 23rd

Manchester United 0 Middlesbrough 1

Frosty Fergie was a man demented. Many more results like this and we'll end up winning nothing this season. Maybe he should have quit while he was ahead, instead of hanging on for another couple of years. But then, fame is an aphrodisiac, as I know only too well myself. And although old Frosty is not exactly in the same celebrity league as me (if you'll pardon the football pun) I can understand the miserable old git wanting to cling on to his position as a minor public figure for a little while longer.

Sunday March 24th

There was a time when people would come to the house to see me, laden down with Dinkey toys, Smarties and *Bob The Builder* colouring books. Now I appear to be an irrelevance. The most I can expect is a casual wave before they disappear into the lounge with Mum and start talking about that Blasted Baby.

The latest snippet from this salon of squeals is that Mum has decided on a natural birth – no make-up, no lipstick, no eye-shadow.

Monday March 25th

Everyone is talking about the upcoming

World Cup and there is no doubt what is emerging as the most burning, vital, significant and nail-biting issue: which hair-style will Dad adopt? Bookies are quoting 11-4 on the shaven head look while the mullet comes in at 10-1. I really don't care, as long as he doesn't go for a David Seaman. I just don't get that Seaman style. The man's England's No. 1 goalkeeper, for God's sake, a position of pride and prominence. Doesn't he understand that these days pigtails are only worn by street-level drug dealers, nightclub bouncers and rock group roadies?

Tuesday March 26th

She's here! The divine Britney is in London and I was not surprised to read that she had no time to stop and chat to the fans who waited to see her at the West End premiere of her film, *Crossroads*. She must have been rushing for a phone to contact me, although I kept my mobile on all night and heard nothing. Maybe she's lost the number.

Wednesday March 27th

Still nothing from Britney. However, no one understands better than me the demands of Superstardom. I expect she's busy.

Thursday March 28th

A whole team of designers arrived at Beckingham Palace today to start getting ready for the World Cup party. I haven't seen so many young men with highlighted hair and tight trousers since we went to a barbecue round at John Elton's place in the summer.

Friday March 29th

Apparently the party has a Japanese theme. I hope they don't serve that disgusting sushi stuff which Mum eats and Dad pretends to before stuffing it in his trouser pockets. Some of his slacks are beginning to whiff like a whaling fleet.

Meanwhile, the Blasted Baby is getting the kind of VIP treatment which has me more and more unsettled. Mum and Dad have booked a £60,000 suite at the Portland Hospital so that when the kid arrives it can become acclimatised to immediate luxury.

And they may be asking John Elton to be the Godfather. Now, I've seen *The Godfather* on video. He's this Italian bloke who talks as though he's got his mouth full of toilet paper and he keeps having people killed. It doesn't seem at all a suitable role for such a sensitive soul as John Elton. On the other hand, I have noticed that, at parties, John Elton goes up to both men and women, kisses them passionately and says: 'Ooh, baby, I love you to death.' Being loved to death by John Elton? Now, that's an offer I really *could* refuse.

Saturday March 30th

A tailor arrived today to measure me for the

Japanese outfit I'm going to wear for the party. It's supposed to be a surprise, and as The Vultures of Fleet Street are already hovering for the slightest morsel of info about the party I will tell you only that it tends towards the traditional. Bit of a waste, really. If they'd kept any of my old nappies, I could have gone as a sumo wrestler.

Sunday March 31st

With the World Cup in mind, Dad's been learning some Japanese jokes from his football mates. His favourite is the one about the Jewish kamikaze pilot who crashed his plane on his brother's scrapyard. I bet that will have 'em rolling in the aisles in Osaka.

Having been told that bowing low is a mark of respect in Japan, Dad has been practising at home. The problem is that every time he leans forward he head-butts the mirror.

APRIL 2002

Monday April 1st

Oh love, how elusive is thy fleeting pleasure. The beautiful Britney has flown back to America without so much as a message for me. I expect her lovely head is still in a whirl over the way she was treated by that swine Justin Timberhead. I've posted another letter up the chimney telling Britney that I'll always be here for her. And this time I've stuck on a stamp from the Postman Pat outfit that I got for Christmas, so it's bound to get there.

Tuesday April 2nd

Deportivo La Coruña 0 Manchester United 2

Bad news from Spain. Dad was taken off on a stretcher after injuring his ankle. With the World Cup only a couple of months away, he can't afford any serious knocks. The papers are treating it as the worst national crisis since the Second World War and it was all over the late night news on TV. Poor old Trevor McDonald was almost in tears and I half expected them to start playing funereal music in the background.

Wednesday April 3rd

Phew, what a relief. Dad flew back to England limping a bit, but he's going to be all right. Once again the nation can sleep soundly in its bed.

Thursday April 4th

Dad's still up in Manchester having treatment

but he phoned to say he'd be home tomorrow and he's brought me some prezzies from Spain.

Friday April 5th

It's great having Dad back, but the presents were a bit of a letdown. It's hard to get excited over a straw sombrero, a pair of maracas and a leather donkey. Mum wasn't over the moon with her flamenco doll either.

Saturday April 6th

Mum's always going on about how important it is to protect Dad's image, so she threw a right wobbly at a shopping centre in Kent when she came across a store selling what she insisted was a fake signed photograph of Dad. She went in and tore the shopkeeper off a right strip and insisted he remove it from the window. I daresay she's right. But how you can spot a forged 'X' is a bit of a mystery to me.

Sunday April 7th

We were out in the Merc today when we passed a clock that said 10.30. A little further on there was another clock that said 10.15. 'That's odd,' said Dad. 'We must be going the wrong way.'

Monday April 8th

The bloke who used to manage the Spice Girls is talking about reuniting the girls to mark their tenth anniversary. I dunno how Mum's going to feel about that. The idea of she and The Big Bad Evil Ginger One getting back together seems about as likely as Paul McCartney doing a duet with Yoko Ono.

Tuesday April 9th

There's a picture of the beautiful Britney in the paper, laughing and joking and looking really happy on a beach in Florida. She must have got my letter.

Wednesday April 10th

Manchester United 3 Deportivo La Coruña 2

Oh no, not again. Dad went down after a really nasty tackle and it looks as though he could be badly injured.

Thursday April 11th

Seeing the size of the headlines in today's papers, you'd think that the end of the world was imminent. But it's worse than that. Dad's broken a bone in his foot and it looks as though he could be out of the World Cup.

Friday April 12th

Dad has brought the nation to its knees. Displaying its usual good taste, the *Sun* printed a picture of Dad's naked left foot on the front page and invited everyone to say a prayer for it so it can get better quickly. No doubt the churches across the land will be full on Sunday, praying to that Great Healer in the sky. 'Our Physiotherapist, who art in Heaven ... '

Understandably, Dad's always had a fear of serious injury and whenever he's had to have treatment in the past he's always got into long conversations with the Manchester United physio about the effects of serious knocks. The physio once asked him: 'What would you do if you broke your leg in three places?'

Dad said: 'I'd never go into them three places again.'

Saturday April 13th

Mum responded magnificently to Dad's injury crisis. She's been on the phone all day trying to find out if Gucci do designer crutches.

Sunday April 14th

Apparently that Justin Timberhead is trying to get back with the beautiful Britney, sending her roses and love poems. Ignore him

Britney. Your only true love is right here in Hertfordshire. I long for the day when you can come over and play with my Tonka trucks.

Monday April 15th

Dad's famous foot dominates our every waking hour and it is even having an educational effect. A week ago, half the country couldn't pronounce 'metatarsal'. Now they're bandying the word around like Harley Street surgeons.

Tuesday April 16th

People in Japan are so dismayed by the prospect of Dad not going there for the World Cup that they are making little birds out of folded paper so Dad's foot will get better. Apparently, Japanese tradition says that if you fold 1,000 birds, you can make a wish come true. With the beautiful Britney in mind, I think I'll start folding a few myself.

Wednesday April 17th

It can't be a coincidence that it was tackles by two Argentinean players that led to Dad's recent injuries – the knock on the ankle in Spain and now this broken bone. Mum says it's probably their way of getting back at us for the Falklands. Yeah, those Argies are a nasty lot. I expect the papers in Buenos Aires are showing pictures of Dad's injured foot underneath the headline: 'Gotcha!'

If only Maggie Thatcher were still at No. 10. I bet she'd respond to this outrage by sending a gunboat or something.

Thursday April 18th

Dad managed to hobble down the hall and opened the door to the postman today. 'I'm sorry to trouble you,' said the mailman, 'but I have a package here and I'm not quite sure whether it's for you or not. The name is obliterated.'

'In that case it's definitely not for me,' said Dad. 'My name is Beckham.'

Friday April 19th

Of course, Dad is not the only Beckham in the headlines. In common with the Princes of the realm and other such revered dignitaries, my own future is a topic which continues to evoke widespread discussion and speculation. Mum said on TV that she doesn't want me to grow up to be a singer, she'd prefer me to be a footballer. Personally, I wouldn't mind being a singer. It would be nice to have one in the family.

Saturday April 20th

I told Dad he shouldn't be driving with his bad foot, but he insisted on taking the wheel of the Merc when we went to the local shops. And what happened? We had a prang with another car. Fortunately I was strapped in my top-of-the-range bullet-proof baby seat with the Louis Vuitton upholstery so I was unhurt. But that's the trouble with parents. They never listen.

Sunday April 21st

The other Japanese joke which Dad has learned for the World Cup is the one about the Tokyo firm which specialised in making tinier and tinier mobile phones. They were so successful, they moved to smaller premises. Dad doesn't really get that one, but as everyone else laughed when he heard it he thinks it's great.

Monday April 22nd

Dad's sleeping in a sealed low-oxygen tent at night in the hope that his foot heals more quickly. When he's not looking, I crawl inside and pretend I'm an astronaut. It's brilliant. And the tent really works. I had a pimple on my bum and it disappeared overnight.

Tuesday April 23rd

Dad has had another tattoo – the Roman numerals VII in the inside of his forearm. People think it's because he wears No. 7 on his football shirt. But why the Roman numbers? Maybe we're moving to Italy. Personally I think he started to spell out 'Victoria' for the tattooist and abandoned it when someone pointed out that he'd put in one 'I' too many.

Wednesday April 24th

Dad's injury was on the agenda of a cabinet meeting at 10 Downing Street and even the Queen was heard discussing it at a Windsor reception. Maybe that's what they mean by putting the nation on a war footing. Ha, ha! (That's a joke, geddit?)

Thursday April 25th

Mum has started house hunting for another

place in Cheshire because she thinks our penthouse will be too small when the Blasted Baby arrives. How she can be so insensitive as to worry about the welfare of a child who isn't even born while we are all engrossed in something as important as Dad's foot is beyond me.

Friday April 26th

Sounds as though Mum and Dad's World Cup Party is going to be a swanky affair. The invitations say the dress code is 'white tie and diamonds'. I'll have to ask Dad if I can borrow a pair of his earrings.

Saturday April 27th

The commercialisation of the Beckham name continues apace, and though at times I find it a tad undignified, I must admit it brings in considerable amounts of wonga. Mum's made a telly advert for Walkers crisps in which she appears as Queen Victoria. They were going to film it at our Hertfordshire mansion, but they must have thought it was a bit too grand for them, so in the end they used some inferior gaff called Blenheim Palace instead, which probably saved them a bundle of dough. I just hope it doesn't turn out to be too tacky a setting and make Mum look cheap.

Sunday April 28th

Browsing through Virgin Records' website on my state-of-the-art, super-thin trillion-megabyte laptop, I noticed that they don't even mention the former biggest band in the world which made them squillions of pounds. I speak, of course, of the Spice Girls. How fleeting fame can be. Except, of course, for true Superstars like myself, whose popularity shows no signs of waning. Only this morning I was involved in a scuffle with some fans trying to grab a lock of my hair while Dad was in the newsagent's collecting his *Beano*.

Monday April 29th

My celebrity standing has reached the stage where I am being mobbed in Mothercare. I have been practising my autograph in crayon on my bedroom wall, which hasn't gone down too well.

Meanwhile, the papers say scientists have been analysing Dad's free kicks and they reckon that they reach up to 80mph and swerve 2m in flight. Their conclusion: 'Beckham's brain must be computing very detailed trajectory calculations in a few seconds.' Can this be the same Beckham brain that takes several minutes to decide which boot goes on which foot?

Tuesday April 30th

Bayer Leverkusen 1 Manchester United 1

This result means United are out of the European cup and Frosty Fergie is in severe danger of winning no silverwave at all this season, a prospect which has left him with a facial expression resembling a well-used face flannel.

Elsewhere, Mum's beginning to show a bump in her belly, which apparently confirms that the Blasted Baby is on its way. I did suggest she cancel the order and send it back, what with us being so busy with Dad's foot and everything, but she said it's too late.

Some child expert wrote an article in the paper saying: 'The concern is that Brooklyn is going to feel displaced, having had the lion's share of the attention. When people visit and make a fuss of the new baby, it will make a big difference if they make a fuss of Brooklyn as well.' Damned right, Professor. And if I don't get that attention, you just watch my daily tantrum output switch into overdrive.

MAY
2002

Wednesday May 1st

Workmen arrived at Beckingham Palace to erect a huge marquee in the grounds for Mum and Dad's World Cup party. The tent is bigger than our house and I don't know what they'll do with it afterwards. Maybe they could turn it into a hostel for asylum seekers and start up a shuttle service direct to the Channel Tunnel. The neighbours would just love that.

Thursday May 2nd

Dad's birthday. He's got so much stuff that I didn't know what to get him. In the end I settled for a pair of monogrammed Versace socks. Now, when he looks under the table, he'll be able to tell which feet are his.

Friday May 3rd

Dad's been test-driving a new £166,000 Bentley and I hope he gets it because we are getting a bit low on cars. All we've got left is the Ferrari, the Lincoln Navigator, the BMW 5X and the Mercedes SLK50. That's not even enough to drive a different one every day of the week.

Saturday May 4th

That Justin Timberhead is lower than a snake's belly. Now that he has had no success in getting back with the beautiful, bounteous Britney, I hear he has been putting it about to someone on a plane that she is not a virgin after all. The man's a bounder, and I shall nail him with my Star Wars lightsabre if he ever gets within zapping distance of Beckingham Palace. On the other hand I could do something even nastier to him with the aid of my Harry Potter outfit. Yeah, that's it. I'll zip over to America on my Nimbus Two Thousand Flying Broomstick, don my cloak of invisibility and creep up on him unseen to inflict a little GBH. Then I'll load Britney on the back of the broomstick and bring her back to Britain. What a wizard plan!

Sunday May 5th

In a magazine article, Dad praised my soccer skills, which was nice. But he had to go and spoil it by adding: 'He's got Victoria's musical side in him as well.' Oh come on, Dad. You wouldn't wish that on your worst enemy, let alone your own son.

Monday May 6th

A Bristol pub called The Victoria has done away with the sign that showed the old Queen Victoria and replaced it with a picture of Mum. Further confirmation, I suppose, that the papers are right when they say that we Beckhams are the new royalty. It can only be a matter of time before The Brooklyn Arms opens for business with my own smiling face beaming regally from beneath a glittering golden crown. Or perhaps The Prince Brooklyn, with me in full United kit. The possibilities are endless. It's at times like this I really feel the need for a full-time agent who could negotiate the best deals for me. I'll have to speak to Dad about it.

Tuesday May 7th

Dad's been explaining his attitude towards fashion: 'My style is grungy but I like to look smart too.' Which is why he was pictured at the weekend wearing a £500 Dolce and Gabbana shirt, £150 Moschino jeans and £90 Timberland boots, topped off with £7,000 diamond earrings, a £50,000 diamond ring and a £1,000 gold necklace. Right on, Daddy-o. Gold-plated grunge for the seriously rich. I like it.

Wednesday May 8th

Manchester United 0 Arsenal 1

A good day for throwing my Tonka trucks at the wall. First of all, Arsenal stuff us at Old Trafford to win the Premiership and the Theatre of Dreams turns into a nightmare because it means Arsenal complete the Double and we're left with sweet FA (and I don't mean Football Association) to show for the season.

Even worse, I've just heard that Mum came over all bossy and didn't want Dad appearing in a Pepsi advert with – wait for it – *the beautiful Britney!* Just think, if thats true

Dad could have taken me along to the photo shoot, I'd have been introduced to Britney, it would have been love at first sight and ...

How cruel fate can be. I would mention it to Mum, but I don't want to lay a guilt trip on her simply because she has been responsible for ruining my entire life.

Thursday May 9th

Dad went to 10 Downing Street to meet Tony Blair and chose the occasion to sport a new hairstyle, swept back at the sides and combed together at the back into what is apparently known as a duck's arse. I can't wait to grow one. It will be a sensation at nursery school and one in the eye for that snotty Miss Hawkins, our teacher, who pointedly ignores my Superstar status and instead insists on treating me as just an ordinary kid. She even makes me do up my own buttons.

Friday May 10th

Mum could be right about Dad not really living up to his Superstar status. I mean, he's not afraid to spend a few bob, but he's not really thinking big-time when it comes to splashing out the old wonga on yours truly. I read in the paper that you can rent a California waterpark for £50,000 a day – add another 50,000 big ones for a helicopter and a fleet of limos for all your friends and that'd be what I call cool. It'd certainly beat a crummy cake and a few balloon-bending clowns at a cinema in Manchester. I've cut the story out of the newspaper and stuck it on the door of the toy cupboard where Mum and Dad can see it.

After all, my fourth birthday is only nine months away.

Saturday May 11th

It's not as though Dad couldn't afford a little spoiling. After all, he's finally signed a new contract with Manchester United, for £90,000 a week, though why they couldn't have made it a nice round £100,000, I'll never know. What with his advertising and sponsorship and so on, Dad will be earning around £10 million a year, which isn't bad for a bloke who still has trouble putting his underpants on the right way round.

Sunday May 12th

Spent the day dressed up like a Japanese Samurai warrior for Mum and Dad's World Cup party at Beckingham Palace. The outfit was Mum's idea and she made Dad wear one too. I felt a complete ah so!

There were lots of show business and sports stars there including the England football team and Mum and Dad's pal John

Elton, but I searched in vain for the fabulous Britney, who would surely have outshone them all. A helicopter hovered overhead and I suppose that was to ward of any risk of an aerial attack from The Big Bad Evil Ginger One who was the first *not* to be invited. Mum wore a black leather outfit which made her look like the Princess of Darkness, which I suppose was all part of the plot to fend of the evil powers of the Ginger One. Mum was also larging it up with a diamond necklace which cost more than a million quid, and telling anyone who'd listen just how much it cost, which I found slightly vulgar.

They had an auction for charity at the party and some bloke called Jamie Oliver who apparently has his own TV show paid £29,000 for a pair of Dad's old boots. No wonder they call him The Naked Chump. He could have had a pair of mine for half that price and I'd even have autographed them for free. It would have been a nice piece of change for me, should I suddenly feel the urge to hit Armani-land.

Afterwards everyone stood around slurping champagne and I thought they'd never leave. Then someone suggested that Mum should sing a song and the place emptied within minutes. Which was nice, particularly for Dad because it meant he could enjoy the delights of the bouncy castle all by himself.

But sadly he only had time for a couple of goes as he had to get everything packed for his World Cup trip to the Far East which starts tomorrow. I wish we were going with him, but Mum says it is far too far to travel what with her being pregnant and everything. See what I mean about the Blasted Baby? It's already cramping my style and it's not even been born.

Monday May 13th

Fantastic news! Mum changed her mind at the last minute and we're on our way to spend five days in Dubai with Dad and the England team. We flew in the team plane and I chatted up David Seaman's daughter Georgina, who is some cute babe even if she does share her Dad's dreadful taste in drug-dealer hairstyles.

A few of the England lads went out clubbing when we landed in Dubai and I fancied going with them in search of a little action, but Mum put the block on it. So I settled for a bed-time story, a fizzy orange and an early night.

Tuesday May 14th

Ah, this is the business. Obviously aware of my Superstar status, the hotel in Dubai has given us a great £1,000-a-night suite overlooking the ocean, while the rest of the

England team slum it in mere £250 rooms. They deliver the British newspapers every day, but because this is a Muslim country somebody called Censor has used a black marker pen to cover up all the naughty bits of the Page Three girls in the *Sun*. I didn't find this all that strange, because at home Dad normally draws moustaches on them.

The Foreign Office has obviously been in touch with the Dubai authorities to inform them that I am here, as the hotel is surrounded by armed soldiers and police in case any over enthusiastic fans should try to get to me.

Wednesday May 15th

Donning our new Police shades (a contractual obligation because the makers pay my old man a cool million to wear them), Dad and I hit the Dubai beach today and boy, was I a babe magnet in my *Bob The Builder* swim shorts. The girls were really coming on strong and if I hadn't been holding hands with Dad, who steered me away from their admiring glances, I'd have definitely pulled.

Mum was bigging it up round the pool in her bikini until a bloke wearing a towel and a fan belt on his head came up and asked for her autograph because he thought she was Ginger Spice. Mum went all stony faced and said she was going for a lie down and we haven't seen her since. Even 3,000 miles away from home, it seems, the shadow of The Big Bad Evil Ginger One still stalks the sands of the desert.

Thursday May 16th

There's all kinds of doctors and physiotherapists and medical advisers fussing around the England team to make sure they are in tip-top shape for their games in Japan and Korea. Just out of interest, I got them to run the rule over me and their conclusion was that I was in first-rate condition. However, they stressed how important it was to exercise regularly, so I think I'll have a word with Mum and Dad about getting a personal trainer. Now that the beautiful Britney has entered my life, I need to keep in shape.

The Football Association even have their own psychologist and he says Dad could avoid another ill-tempered World Cup sending-off if he got in touch with his 'feminine side' by following the stories in the Janet and John children's books. Sounds like a good idea. But who's going to read them to him?

Friday May 17th

Time to say goodbye to Dad. He's off to South Korea tomorrow and we're on our way back to England. Mum went all showbizzy on him as they parted and shouted 'Break a leg!' I don't think Sven found that all that funny. But then I don't think Sven finds *anything* funny.

I threw one of those tantrums at the airport because I wanted to go with Dad, but he said I had to stay home and look after Mum, which didn't make much sense to me. Haven't we got guard dogs to do that?

Saturday May 18th

Unlike when we left for Dubai with Dad there were no crowds of fans at the airport when Mum and I got back to London. Which is unusual, because a Superstar like myself normally has to fight his way through the adoring masses. Maybe they didn't know I was coming.

Sunday May 19th

On the other hand, perhaps nobody got a chance to recognise me, because Mum insisted on picking me up and carrying me through the airport. For a Superstar, that's undignified. After all, did you ever see Frank Sinatra being given a piggy back through the arrivals area?

Monday May 20th

Whoops! Mum has parted ways with her latest manager. I don't understand it. I've always found that as long as you do everything the way Mum wants it, you're OK. Where's the problem? Anyway, I don't think she'll really miss him. The way her career is going, there isn't much left to manage.

Tuesday May 21st

Oh no! My worst nightmares have been realised. The beautiful Britney is back together with that treacherous prat Justin Timberhead. A lesser person might be floored by this devastating news, but not me. I will write her another letter professing my undying love the moment I can find my Magic Doodle Sparkle Pen.

Wednesday May 22nd

Dad's foot retains its place as the most famous injured limb in the history of the world, easily outstripping other celebrated physical setbacks such as Lord Nelson's eye, Danniella Westbrook's nose and John Wayne Bobbitt's chopped off you-know-what. The papers are featuring pictures of it, X-rays of it, specialist opinions on it and assorted forecasts about just when it will be back in action. Short of amputating it and putting it in the British Museum, it couldn't possibly achieve any more wide-ranging attention.

Thursday May 23rd

'Becks Is Bouncing Back' said the headlines today, as the papers carried pictures of Dad in South Korea exercising one-footed on a trampoline. Knowing how he is with toys, I bet he didn't let anyone else have a go.

Friday May 24th

Mum's a bit miffed because she hasn't been chosen for the Queen's Golden Jubilee concert at Buckingham Palace next month. Personally, I don't blame Her Majesty. It's supposed to be a happy occasion. The sound of Mum's voice might have stirred up unpleasant memories of a sound the whole nation came to dread during the war: the air raid siren.

Dad was on the phone from Japan tonight. He said there were so many injuries in the England team it was more like a casualty ward than a training camp. I told him to get Sven to give me a call, as the garden gnomes are all fit and could be on the next plane.

Saturday May 25th

They are talking about sending Dad home from Japan if his foot doesn't get better soon, which would be a big disappointment for him, not to mention the entire nation. Mind you, it would be nice to have him back. Kick-abouts on the lawn just aren't the same without him. Mum does her best to fill in, but yesterday me and the garden gnomes beat her 103–0. The score could have been higher but the gnomes weren't playing to their full capacity as they wanted to avoid the risk of injury now they're on standby for Japan.

Sunday May 26th

England 2 Cameroon 2 (friendly)

England are obviously missing Dad, but the good news is that he came on the pitch after the game for a kickabout – and he was able to use the famous left foot. He was smiling all over his face until they started playing Spice Girls songs over the loudspeakers. Then he suddenly came over all pale and queasy and ran for the tunnel.

Incidentally, the chicks are going comp-letely crazy over Dad in Japan, treating him

218

like a combination of Tom Cruise, Brad Pitt and Robbie Williams. I think it unlikely, however, that Dad will succumb to such Oriental blandishments.

Monday May 27th

Oh deep and utter joy. The beautiful Britney must have finally got my letter, because she has dumped that rat Justin Timberhead once and for all. I expect she'll phone me any day now.

Meanwhile the nation continues to go World Cup mad. Even the Archbishop of Canterbury has given vicars permission to change the time of morning services so no one will miss England's opening game against Sweden on Sunday. Not that it will make much difference. Leyton Orient get bigger attendances than the Church of England nowadays.

Mum's planning a bit of a party and has invited people round to watch it on TV, but she can't make up her mind what to wear. She tried on one outfit and said: 'Yuk! If I opened the door in this, they'd mistake me for the cook.'

Not if they stayed for dinner they wouldn't.

Tuesday May 28th

Light the bonfires, ring the bells from the highest steeple, dance in the streets and sing Hallelujah! Dad's foot is better and he will almost certainly play against Sweden. A grateful nation wept for joy and Mum was so excited she had to go out for some shopping therapy. It took three pairs of Gucci shoes and a Dolce and Gabbana trouser suit to calm her down.

Wednesday May 29th

Russia's World Cup Team has been promised that the best player in every match will be given a £60,000 Porsche. I hope Sven

Eriksson can come up with a better bonus than that. A new luxury sports car would hardly be enough incentive for Dad to put his shirt on.

Thursday May 30th

Meanwhile, in a shroud of secrecy not far short of that which surrounded the development of the atomic bomb, Dad's World Cup boots have been flown out to Japan. They went First Class, of course, accompanied by a 20-stone security guard, in case anyone should attempt an act of diabolical sabotage such as putting Supa Glue in the laceholes. The boots are etched with the flag of St. George and the date of the first game, against Sweden. Personally, I think the simple words 'Left' and 'Right' might have been far more useful.

Friday May 31st

Sorry, Dad, I shouldn't have said that last bit about the boots. I take it all back. You are not dim. You are the superest, bestest, most brilliantest Dad in the whole world. Because Mum has just told me that the other thing which you have inscribed on your boots is my name, Brooklyn, spelled out in Japanese script. And that's not all. Some more Japanese writing on the heel is a Ninja warrior's war cry. So it's you, me and the Ninjas, Dad, putting the boot in for England. Banzai, baby! Let's kick some ass!

Saturday June 1st

Well, I'm all ready for tomorrow's match. I've got my England shirt and Adidas have delivered an exact copy of Dad's special World Cup boots, so I really look the part. Just to get in the mood, I went out the back and thrashed the garden gnomes 197–0. Mum drew the line at me having the Cross of St. George dyed into my hair, which is a bit strange when you consider some of the hairstyles she's let Dad get away with. Anyway, if Phoenix Chi comes round tomorrow she's promised to do it with a can of spray paint while Mum's not looking. Phoenix also said she'd bring a six-pack of Boddington's and a couple of smokes which would be great.

Britain has gone World Cup crazy and some churches are actually putting up big TV screens in front of the altar so that the congregation can watch. Even the Queen has sent the team her best wishes. Here one goes, here one goes, here one goes!

Sunday June 2nd

England 1 Sweden 1

I don't know what happened to the Ninjas' war cry but it obviously doesn't work against the Vikings. Dad's brilliant corner led to our first goal but after that we fell apart and the Swedes made us look like turnips. Dad came on the phone from Japan all disappointed and said: 'Maybe the team should have been made up differently.'

'Yes, David,' said Mum. 'You looked really

pale on the telly. Next time, use a darker foundation and a little more eye liner.'

Monday June 3rd

Gloom and doom over the England result, but the government must have known something like that was going to happen because they came up with a brilliant ploy to take the nation's mind off it. They threw this big party for the Queen, who was celebrating her Golden Jubilee. I don't know what a Golden Jubilee is – it sounds a bit like an ice-cream in a fancy wrapper. Anyway, I got all excited when I heard that her celebration was going to be held in the grounds of Beckingham Palace, because I thought it would be an opportunity to open up our back garden for a real fun knees-up after that boring World Cup 'do' for grown-ups which Mum and Dad hosted and where people like John Elton ponced around in ridiculous clothes calling each other 'sweetie'. However, it turned out to be some other gaff called Buckingham Palace, where the Queen lives, which was bit of a let down.

Tuesday June 4th

I watched the Queen's party on television and there seemed to be distinct lack of jelly and ice-cream. It was full of these wrinkly old rock 'n' roll singers and musical has-beens. They included Baby Spice The Deceiver who looked really tarty in a most revealing and unsuitable black dress. To think I could ever have surrendered my heart to such a brazen hussy. True to form, she inisted on sending 'big kisses to William', a sentiment aimed at Prince William, who, like me, is a bit of a babe magnet. I suppose she did that to try and make me jealous. Forget it, Baby. I don't do humiliation.

Wednesday June 5th

Dad said on the phone that he'd been shopping in Japan and bought some brilliant things. I hope he got me a Samurai sword, so I can do some serious damage to that stupid Justin Timberhead if he ever tries to bother the beautiful Britney again. A little light dismemberment courtesy of a razor sharp ceremonial blade would surely have a deterrent effect.

Thursday June 6th

We're playing Argentina in the World Cup tomorrow. If we lose, that Samurai sword might come in handy for Dad and the rest of the England team to commit hari-kari.

Friday June 7th

England 1 Argentina 0

'Don't cry for me, Argentina,
The truth is, we really stuffed you … '
There have been several memorable moments of extreme tension in my life. One was when I took my first step in learning to walk, that split second of teetering into the unknown

when you are not sure if you are going to stand there wobbling or fall flat on your face. Then there was the night I went to bed without a nappy for the first time, lying there sucking my thumb and wondering whether I could stay dry until the morning or wake up in the usual halo of dampness.

But such agonies of apprehension faded into insignificance as I watched Dad take his run-up to take the penalty. His Ninja warrior boots, laced with the spirit of Brooklyn Beckham, raced across the green turf of the Sapporo stadium and then: Wham! The ball was in the net and our little group at Beckingham Palace went potty and Mum started crying and the dogs started barking and I could swear even the garden gnomes were cheering. Goldenballs Beckham had done it again, and when Dad called from Japan later and asked for me, I had to take the phone into the other room for privacy because I realised that this was a unique moment in history, to be compared with the time that the Duke of Wellington phoned home on his mobile with the Waterloo result or when Sir Francis Drake reversed the charges from a coin box on Plymouth Hoe to announce that he had screwed the Spanish Armada. Such momentous occasions are usually marked by a memorable phrase that will echo down through the centuries, such as: 'I came, I saw, I conquered' or 'This was their finest hour'.

Dad's epic overview, as expressed to me, will, I fear, have a somewhat less enduring impact. 'Yeah, it was brilliant, wunnit?' is not exactly the stuff of history.

Saturday June 8th

Forget the knighthood. It is quite obvious that the entire nation would prefer Dad to progress directly to Sainthood, with the Ninja warrior boots enshrined forever alongside the Crown Jewels in the Tower of

London. The phone has not stopped ringing and I am beginning to think that Dad's post-match proclamation might be some kind of historical milestone after all. Every time Mum picks up the phone she says: 'Yeah, it was brilliant, wunnit?' The more you think about it, the more suitable the epitaph becomes.

Sunday June 9th

'Yeah, it was brilliant, wunnit?' The phrase is repeated through every pub and club in the land. It reverberates around the humblest High Street, it resounds in the remotest corner of the country, it is the nation's modern mantra in its hour of victory, pride and deliverance.

'Yeah, it was brilliant, wunnit?'

It's beginning to sound quite Churchillian.

Monday June 10th

'Yeah, it was brilliant, wunnit?' I even heard

it at nursery school today. From the teachers, mostly.

Virgin Records and Mum have gone their separate ways now. They said it was an amicable agreement, although I'd never have described Mum as amicable ... or agreeable.

Tuesday June 11th

Japan has gone Beckham crazy. Dad's picture is plastered all over their papers and kids out there are copying everything, from his earrings to his hairstyle. I was interested to read that I, too, have an enormous following in the Land of The Rising Son. Sorry, make that Sun. Apparently mums model their own children on The Most Famous Toddler in Britain, and they only have to see a picture of me in my *Bob The Builder* T-shirt to go running out to the shops demanding one like it. And no three-year-old's wardrobe is complete without a Manchester United shirt. It conjures up a touching picture of hundreds of thousands of Japanese kids getting up each morning, changing into their M.U. kit and then bowing low in homage before their makeshift bedroom shrines, where fragrant incense perfumes the air and flickering candles light up giant wallposters of my good self, Brooklyn Beckham-San. It is not in my nature to be humble, but I feel very close to it right now.

Meanwhile, Beckham mania continues here at home, too. Requests for Press and TV interviews and photo sessions have flooded in, but I have refused them all. Dad is also getting a lot of attention and this morning Madame Tussaud's pulled a brilliant stunt by erecting their waxwork figure of Dad on an empty pedestal in Trafalgar Square. Police made them take it down, but not before the entire West End had been brought to a halt by honking motorists and cheering crowds, who were gazing in awe upon the likeness of our national hero. I wouldn't be surprised if they take old Nelson down from his column and put Dad's statue up there instead. Or maybe they could have them side by side: Nelson's Eye and Beckham's Foot, symbols of worldwide supremacy. Rule Britannia!

It's England v Nigeria tomorrow, and we need a draw to secure a place in the finals. I have set my *Bob The Builder* alarm clock for 7am. Can't wait!

Wednesday June 12th

England 0 Nigeria 0

Yeah, it was mediocre, wunnit? Still, ritual suicide with the Samurai sword won't be necessary. Dad and the lads are through to the next round of the World Cup, which is all that really matters. And the Argies are out and on their way home, which is a real bonus. They'll probably have to be smuggled into Buenos Aires by a back door to avoid being lynched by their loyal fans. Oh no, the Argies don't like it up 'em, Captain Mainwaring.

Dad was on the phone saying he'd love to go out and celebrate but he daren't set foot outside the hotel because of the hordes of Japanese admirers who follow him everywhere. I know the feeling, Dad. I have given up going to Sainsbury's for similar reasons. The last time I went, there was a near-riot when a group of schoolgirls spotted me at the checkout and the bodyguards had to whisk me to safety through the 10 Items or Less lane, which luckily was clear at the time. Unfortunately my newly bought Kit Kat got badly crushed in the process, but I suppose that is a small price to pay when one has just survived a life-threatening experience.

Thursday June 13th

England expects that every man will do his duty. The nation has gone all super-patriotic over the World Cup and you'd think we were going into battle rather than warming up for another football match. We play Denmark on

Saturday and I hope that Dad and the lads can bring home the bacon (that's a joke, geddit?).

Friday June 14th

Dad was on the phone from Japan tonight. He's all hyped up about this match with Denmark tomorrow, but I really don't know what he's worried about. Those magic Ninja warrior boots, imbued with the spirit of Brooklyn Beckham, will surely do the business against the Vikings. England expects, Dad. Cry God for Harry, England and St. George! (I don't know who this Harry bloke is, but let's give him a cheer anyway.) Dad said he'd give us a wave on the telly from Japan. Great, Dad. As Nelson himself might say, I'll keep an eye out for you. (Apologies for these awful jokes which keep slipping in, but I have been listening to this CD which Dad had for his birthday: *The Best of Bernard Manning*.)

Saturday June 15th

England 3 Denmark 0

Well, we gave them a Viking good hiding
(sorry about that – it's the Bernard Manning
influence again). Dad and the lads romped
home against the Danes and are through to
the quarter finals of the World Cup. The
sacred Ninja warrior boots, laced with the
spirit of my good self, set up the first goal
from a corner and Dad was at his most
eloquent when he phoned from Japan :

'Yeah, it was brilliant, wunnit?'

Naturally enough, the nation went potty,
but not as crazy as the Japanese, who now
look up to Dad as some kind of God. He's so
taken with the reception he's getting out there
that he's even mentioned the possibility of
going to play in Japan. Dad, a word of
caution here. *Don't do it!* The prospect of
eating sushi sandwiches for the rest of my life
is not one I relish, and tuning in to Saturday

sport on the telly in Tokyo and finding it filled with seven hours of Sumo wrestling also doesn't thrill me. No, Dad. If you're looking for a move, America is the place to be.

Speaking of which, I see that Justin Timberhead has been talking about life without the beautiful Britney and says: 'I know what it's like to have a broken heart now. You get to the point where you cry yourself to sleep at night.' Yeah, Justin, so now you know – love hurts. Still no word from Britney, by the way, despite my putting a Postman Pat first-class stamp on my last letter. But she's on tour right now, so I expect she's busy.

Monday June 17th

Japanese Rain 1 Dad's Hairstyle 0

The papers are full of pictures of Dad looking totally bedraggled during Saturday's match, with his feathery Mohican look almost flattened by the non-stop rain, so that it finished up looking more like a crash helmet than £300-worth of barbering. Even if he had buckets full of gel and a tanker load of hairspray, the chances of him being able to resurrect his hairstyle and restore it to its former glory are pretty slim. So his personal hairdresser is jetting out from Britain even as I write, comb and scissors at the ready, to ensure that Captain Marvel will look his brilliant best again when he leads the team out against the mighty Brazil on Friday. I suppose it's the modern equivalent of St. George sending for his personal sword-sharpener before he slew the dragon.

Tuesday June 18th

Pleeeeeees, Mum, oh pleeeees, pleeeees, pleeeees. I promise I'll be a good boy, and I won't keep asking for ice-cream, and I won't keep kicking the seat in front on the aeroplane, and I'll even do pee-pees before I leave the house so you don't have to stop the car on the way to the airport. And, as a special concession, I won't even throw any tantrums. Pleeees, Mum, can we go? Oh, come on, pleeees!

Forgive my hysteria, dear diary, but I am embarked upon a campaign to get to Japan to see Dad play against Brazil on Friday. After all, my heart is already out there, laced for ever into Dad's Ninja warrior boots, which will no doubt to the business against the sons of the Samba.

All the England team's wives and girl friends have been invited to fly out and although there is no mention of kids, as the captain's wife I'm sure Mum could pull rank and lean on Sven to give me the go ahead. Does Mum not realise the worldwide importance of this forthcoming event? Does she not understand that Britain's Most Famous Toddler simply must be there?

But, wouldn't you know it, it's the Blasted Baby which is proving the problem. They don't think the doctors will allow Mum to fly because she's pregnant. Now, look, I don't want to get too heavy with a kid that's not even born, but the fact is that this Blasted Baby is screwing up my entire life. I mean, didn't the little airhead even look at its diary before deciding to set off in our direction? Couldn't it have seen that it's journey clashed with the World Cup?

When Dad comes on the phone tonight I'm going to get him to ask Sven if they can arrange for the FA to provide a minder to accompany me out to Japan. Mum will be disappointed to be left at home, but she should have thought of that when she crept into the gazebo with Dad all those months ago. Anyway, the guard dogs can look after her – it's about time they started earning their Chum.

Yeah, Mum, I'll tell you what I want, what I really, really want. *I want to go to Japan to see dad.*

Wednesday June 19th

Waaaaaaaaagh! Shreeeeeeek! Yaaaaaaaa! Sob. Sob. Gulp. Sob. Intake of breath. Waaaaaagh! Shreeeeeek! Yaaaaaaa!

That, dear diary, is the sound of me in full tantrum mode. And who could blame me for such a heel-drumming display of protest? I turn on the telly and there are the wives and girlfriends of the England team *plus kids* flying out to Japan. Oh no, this is turning into a nightmare. We are on the verge of sporting history, one of those events that will surely qualify for the category of do-you-remember-where-you-were-when ... And where will I be when Dad and the lads do the business with the boys from Brazil in Shizouka? Cheering them on from a VIP box? Sitting alongside Sven, giving him a hint or two about tactics? Not at all. I'll be 6,000 miles away in Hertfordshire, watching some grey-haired cove called Des Lynam explain it all to me on the telly. I've pulled every trick in the toddlers' book to try to get myself out there. Tantrummed. Sulked. Banged doors. Kicked the cat. Thrown teddy at the wall. Overturned my chocolate milk in anger. I've pleaded with Mum for her to let grandma and grandad take me out. But all I get from her is: 'We'll see.'

Now, I know all about 'we'll see': Mum, can I have a motorbike? 'We'll see.' Mum, can I stay up late to watch *Only Fools and Horses*? 'We'll see.' Can I have diamond earrings like Dad? 'We'll see.'

Look, I've been a fully grown three-year-old long enough to know that 'we'll see' means a straight no, but this is the answer that grown-ups give to kids in the hope that we'll eventually forget about whatever it is that we want.

Thursday June 20th

Despair is everywhere. The point of no

return has been passed and even if Mum has a last-minute change of heart there's no way I can get to Japan in time for tomorrow's match. Me and teddy sobbed ourselves to sleep last night, although teddy's distress may also have been connected with the various minor injuries he suffered yesterday when I slammed him against the wall (one eye remains permanently wonky). Sorry, ted.

The thing is, in years to come we'll be sitting around talking about the day England played Brazil in Japan and someone like David Seaman's daughter will be able to say: 'Yeah, I was there.' Then they'll all look at me, The Captain's Son, and all I'll be able to mumble is: 'Yeah, I saw it on the telly.'

Well, I just hope this Blasted Baby is a quick learner when it arrives. Because as soon as it knows how to listen, I'm going to give it a right earholing about how it ruined the greatest day of my life.

Friday June 21st

England 1 Brazil 2

Huh, Georgina Seaman may well be able to say 'I was there.' But the question is, where was her Dad? To be more precise, where was he at exactly 8.24am, when Brazil scored the winner? The answer, unfortunately, is that he was several miles off his line, back-pedalling like an Italian tank commander in the Second World War as Ronaldinho's free kick sailed over his head and sent us out of the World Cup. I blame Sven for playing David Seaman in the first place. Apart from his objectionable hairstyle, the man is ancient – 38 years old, which is almost 13 times as old as I am. I don't even expect my pet tortoise to live that long.

Mum was in tears when Dad came on the phone from Japan. I think she realised she dropped a clanger in not letting me fly out for the game. After all, it's one thing to have the spirit of Brooklyn Beckham laced into Dad's Ninja warrior boots. But if Britain's Most Famous Toddler, The Captain's Son, had been there in person, who knows what kind of inspirational karma I could have exerted on Dad and the lads?

Saturday June 22nd

A nation mourns. Always one to know how to cope with such a crisis, Mum took a stretch limo up to Mayfair for a £300 hairdo. When the football-mad stylist asked how she'd like it cut, she said: 'In complete silence.'

Sunday June 23rd

Dad's home! I don't care what happened in Japan, he'll always be a hero to me. Especially 'cos he's brought me home a bag full of brilliant new video games and a complete Samurai warrior outfit which should cause quite a stir when I wear it on my next outing to Tesco's.

Monday June 24th

Forget the World Cup. There is news of something much more important. My beloved Britney is free at last and rumours are she is looking for love. Talking about the bust-up of her relationship with Justin Timberhead, she explained: 'I haven't really dated anyone since. I am the type of person who can't go from a serious relationship and then just start dating someone else straight away.'

I understand, Britney baby. But whenever you're ready, I'm here.

Tuesday June 25th

More great news on the Britney front. She's just been voted the No. 1 celebrity in the whole wide world. I've written her a congratulatory note and popped it up the chimney so she should get it in a couple of days.

Dear Britney,

I don't need no silly old magazine poll to know that you are the bestest girl in the whole world. My Dad brought me a Samurai warrior outfit from Japan and I will send you a picture of me wearing it.
Love,
Brooklyn Beckham.

Wednesday June 26th

Dad appears to be labouring under a complete delusion regarding my feelings about the arrival of the Blasted Baby. He told a newspaper: 'Brooklyn knows he is going to have some new company fairly soon and he is obviously very excited about it. But he also says he is not too bothered whether he gets a brother or sister to play with.'

Wrong, Daddy-o. I await the impending birth with about as much enthusiasm as I would summon up for a course of anti-rabies injections. And if I want something to play with, I'll whistle up one of the dogs.

Thursday June 27th

Dad's still pretty gloomy over the World Cup defeat. Last night I noticed that he left a whole Jammie Dodger uneaten on his plate, which is a certain sign that he's seriously upset. I tried to cheer him up with a new knock-knock joke that I'd heard at nursery school.

Knock knock.
Who's there?
Bet.
Bet who?
Bet You Wish David Seaman Had Saved That Free Kick.

Strange, Dad didn't seem to find that one all that funny.

Friday June 28th

Dad was invited to a White Tie and Tiara ball at John Elton's place, but he decided not to go because he didn't fancy spending the entire evening fending off people who wanted to commiserate with him over the World Cup result. I don't blame him. John Elton's pals tend to be a sensitive bunch of flowers and Dad obviously didn't relish the prospect of a procession of tight-trousered young men putting their arms around him and sobbing.

Saturday June 29th

It's now been a year since we moved into Beckingham Palace and although it's a brilliant house I've always had the feeling that, as the home of Superstars, it still lacked that certain something. I mean, we have all the essential celebrity status symbols such as a snooker room, gymnasium, swimming pool, recording studio and state-of-the-art security system. But this morning a letter from Hertfordshire council provided the missing link.

Sunday June 30th

We're getting our own helicopter landing pad!

The letter from the council was planning permission, so we'll soon be equipped for Celebrityland high-fliers to chopper in to Beckingham Palace. Just think, Santa Claus will be able to drop from the clouds on Christmas Eve, that Mohammed Al Fayed bloke might whirlybird in with some more stuffed brown envelopes, and Dad's hairdresser can answer emergency calls by landing right there on the back lawn next to the garden gnomes.

And (dare I mention it?) one day the beautiful Britney herself might descend on us like an angel from the skies, ducking to avoid the spinning rotor blades of the helicopter as she races across the grass into my arms like a slow-motion sequence in a Hollywood love story.

In the wonderful world of Brooklyn Beckham, things can only get better.